The Thief's Funeral

The Thief's Funeral

THE BOOK REVIEW ANTHOLOGY OF SHORT FICTION

EDITED BY
SUCHARITA SENGUPTA
CHANDRA CHARI
UMA IYENGAR

ALEPH

in association with

ALEPH

ALEPH BOOK COMPANY
An independent publishing firm
promoted by *Rupa Publications India*

First published in India in 2024
by Aleph Book Company
7/16 Ansari Road, Daryaganj
New Delhi 110 002

This anthology copyright © Aleph Book Company 2024
Copyright in the stories © The Book Review
Literary Trust 2024

All rights reserved.

This is a work of fiction. Names, characters, places,
and incidents are either the product of the authors'
imagination or are used fictitiously and any resemblance
to any actual persons, living or dead, events or locales is
entirely coincidental.

No part of this publication may be reproduced,
transmitted, or stored in a retrieval system, in any form
or by any means, without permission in writing from
Aleph Book Company.

ISBN: 978-81-19635-98-6

1 3 5 7 9 10 8 6 4 2

Printed in India.

This book is sold subject to the condition that it shall
not, by way of trade or otherwise, be lent, resold, hired
out, or otherwise circulated without the publisher's prior
consent in any form of binding or cover other than that
in which it is published.

CONTENTS

Introduction — vii
SUCHARITA SENGUPTA

Feast of the Sacrifice — 1
PARESH TIWARI

Not a Day for Outings — 9
ARMAAN VERMA

Beating Loneliness — 20
JUANITA KAKOTY

Saved by the Terrorists — 30
RANJAN PAL

Lata and the Mermaid — 39
C. JAYANTI

The Anklet on Her Left Foot — 49
IPSITA MISHRA

Spirited Nights — 57
VIKRAM BALAGOPAL

The Smell of Joipur — 64
LEISANGTHEM GITARANI DEVI

Reflections on a Common Journey — 76
NEERA KASHYAP

The Pimp SUBHASH CHANDRA	86
Megalomania JOBETH ANN WARJRI	95
The Patient SOURABH MUKHERJEE	103
The Tenant RACHITA RAJ	117
When the Sun Falls from the Sky ANURADHA VIJAYAKRISHNAN	123
The Thief's Funeral MOHAMMAD SALMAN	135
A New Home for Bhainsa MADHULIKA LIDDLE	148
Return to Life MUDDASIR RAMZAN	161
Her Day SANTANU DAS	168
The Pumpkin Eaters SHALIM HUSSAIN	173
Notes on the Contributors	182

INTRODUCTION

In 2020, The Book Review Literary Trust announced a short story competition. In the midst of viral rampage and global devastation, we received an overwhelming response. We are pleased to present *The Thief's Funeral: The Book Review Anthology of Short Fiction,* including the winning entries from this competition.

The winning entry, 'Megalomania' by Jobeth Ann Warjri, is a casual peek into the mind of a predator. In a brilliant study of power play, Warjri's spare prose evokes the delusional self-confidence of the hunter and the subtle terror of the hunted. The first runner up, Armaan Verma's 'Not a Day for Outings' captures the bittersweet complexity of a single mother's relationship with her daughter. Fractious immaturity coexists with a deep, mature bond of love, yet every mother and daughter know fully well that the route from one to the other is painfully confusing. The second runner-up, Santanu Das's 'Her Day', is a portrait of an ageing female protagonist, evoking acute pathos as she witnesses the bonfire of her vanities.

Mohammad Salman's short story 'The Thief's Funeral' is an allegory that walks us through the collective superficiality of our society, forcing our gaze upon our inconsistencies and hypocrisy. Injustice is not a cataclysmic event, but a series of quotidian habits, a perverse life force animating our worst human impulses. Slivers of sense may yet rescue us from this purgatory, as the story reminds us of hope. Even so, hope is a currency hard to come by. In Anuradha Vijaykrishnan's 'When the Sun Falls from the Sky', hope is a chimera. When a child can see through this veil, every dream's ending is trauma. 'Reflections of a Common Journey' by Neera Kashyap draws out these very dark corners of lovelessness and brutality, wrought upon a child by his own family.

Barbarities also populate the public sphere, with crime being rife. Ranjan Pal, in 'Saved by Terrorists', tells a morbid tale connecting crimes in far corners of the earth, one ironically blending into the other. In 'The Tenant' by Rachita Raj a young city woman is haunted to death. Not all hauntings are unwelcome though. Vikram Balagopal fuses magic and desire in 'Spirited Nights'. Female queer desire is still grappling with being in the realm of the forbidden. Only under darkness does it find free rein with an imaginary consort.

After all is said and done, we are left with those two hoary chestnuts—faith and doubt. This world is not enough to find satisfactory answers to this debate. Muddasir Ramzan takes us to outer space in 'Return to Life', where the interplay between science, faith, and doubt continues to follow the world-weary protagonist.

These short stories, and the remainder in the anthology, showcase voices that continue to interrogate the human condition, which is universal and variegated, all at once. The tales have emerged from a range of social, cultural, and cognitive landscapes. The emotions felt upon reading them, however, are a testament to the common concerns of humankind. The stories bring into sharp relief messy and uncomfortable inner worlds and their tension with norms and morals. Loneliness is stark, despair is rife. No one is spared. Not the old woman caught in the cycle of perpetuating generational trauma, nor the rich lady witnessing destitution from afar. Women continue to bear the whiplash of patriarchy, which manages to reappear time and again in horrific ways. The maddening dance between sexual repression and assault leaves one with the feeling of being on a vomit-inducing roller coaster ride. Religion and caste bear down upon the most vulnerable, the stories bearing witness to the astonishing pathways of calumny, bizarre yet very real. Greed appears in the world with a rather light touch, as easy as breathing. The only time it becomes a problem is when there isn't enough to sell, and so the economy of absurdity becomes, well, even more absurd in the service of consumerism.

Running through this anthology is the uniting thread of terror. From the terror of looking at one's face that the world deems to not be pretty enough, to the terror of finding ways to dispose of cattle without losing one's life. From the terror of not being able to trust fellow humans, to the terror of not being able to be oneself fully and freely. Perhaps the fear in the stories is a reflection of the zeitgeist—the assault on the self and communities by everything ranging from pathogens to political leaders, and everything in between.

The anthology does more than merely privilege fear. In the snappy format that is the short story, it compels us to take a hard look at the kind of society we inhabit. Literature is the denunciation of the times in which one lives, as Nobel Prize winner Camilo José Cela astutely pointed out. We hope that the stories will not only introduce the reader to new writing, but also do what all good writing does—make one think and feel.

The competition was the brainchild of Ambassador Kiran Doshi, career diplomat, educationist, and award-winning author of several novels and short stories. Ambassador Doshi graciously sponsored the prize for this competition, and also took a keen interest in judging the entries. His demise in early 2023 has been a loss to both diplomacy and the world of literature. While we are deeply saddened that he is not here to see the anthology in publication, we are honoured that he was the progenitor and part of the process.

Finally, this work owes an immense debt of gratitude to Chandra Chari, Uma Iyengar, David Davidar, Adnan Farooqui, and Aienla Ozukum, without whose wisdom, support, and contribution, the volume would not have seen the light of day.

—Sucharita Sengupta

FEAST OF THE SACRIFICE
PARESH TIWARI

The sun slipped behind the moss splotched onion dome of the mosque. Thirty-nine rock doves fluttered down the spire on to the square patch of concrete below. Two lanes to the right, at the gurgling mouth of a brick-lined drain, squatted Arif. Biting his fingernails. Muttering under his breath. Entreating the djinns and the faeries in a tongue that he didn't even understand. He was a frail boy of eleven, perhaps twelve, with a mop of unruly hair, a nose too big for his face and coal eyes sunk into a sloping forehead.

For now, those eyes were fixed on Basu, waiting. Everything else faded to the periphery of time; the lengthening shadow of the matchbox house with three windows and pale blue walls, the changing shape of the gang of boys—now a deer, now leopard, now hyena—circling the pair nervously, and the ice-cream wallah who had stopped his tricycle eight paces short of them. The noon breeze held its breath as Basu—holding a green translucent marble between his fingers, grey muslin shirt clinging to his back—wiped away a rivulet of sweat and sat on his haunches. Resting his left palm on the road, he steadied himself and contemplated the white marble at the edge of a rough chalk circle.

One such evening, not so long ago, Arif had held it against the sun and studied its pattern, a wave mid-crash, frozen inside a drop of glass and stars scattered around it.

He had never been to Mumbai, but his Mamu had told him about Chowpatty and how the sky there lowered its spread of stars and dipped it into the waves. Arif had always wanted to visit the beach, but until that happened, this tiny white marble was his succour. His own slice of sky plunging into the waves.

Time is molten wax pooling in a hollow under the wick. It is the flap of a fledgling's wings wrestling gravity on its first flight. Time, today for Arif, marched with deliberate measured steps. Later, if you had asked him, he would have recalled the precise trajectory of the green marble and the sound of glass hitting glass. He would have described with exactness how the gang's jubilant whoops splintered the air, or the tilt of Basu's head as he turned to look at him. He may even have told you the number of steps Basu took before bending down to pick up his winnings—Arif's slice of sky plunging into the waves. What he would have never been able to say is how he reached home that evening.

Back home, within the peeling walls of 314, Agha Meer ki Dyodhi, Abbu sat with the Sunday edition of *Avadhnama*, turning its limp pages with detachment.

Ammi shuffled by in the small L-shaped kitchen, boiling tea leaves in a concoction of milk, cardamom, and sugar. Any other day, he would have stopped by the kitchen and gobbled a samosa or two. He would have even talked awhile with his mother. Miming his best throw and producing, with the flourish of a magician, the marbles he had won that day. In a family of four men, where the primary job of Mrs Kazim was to be a provider of food, tea, clean clothes, and no-nonsense sex, these few minutes were the high point of her day.

'Today I have made your favourite tamarind chutney

Feast of the Sacrifice

along with the samosas,' she called out only to find her voice gasp for breath before drowning in the rush of rubber slippers up the stone stairs.

Arif banged shut the door to his room and flopped down on the floor. He shared this room with his two elder brothers. The cracked walls were held together with posters of cricket and movie stars—a young and curly haired batsman Sachin Tendulkar dominated the walls. In just a few years since joining the national team, this seventeen-year-old had become 'the one' that everyone aspired to be. Arif himself had taken a shine to cricket since Sachin joined the Indian team. He had even gone to the nearby cricket field with his brothers, but his cricket aspirations were cut short by a leather ball that found a spot on his ankle. The impact had left him limping for weeks and he didn't bother with the game again. On another wall was the poster of a movie star in a black vest. The words 'Salman' printed in a bright yellow across the width of his gleaming biceps. The photo of his eldest brother in the same haircut and a similar black vest was sellotaped to a corner of the poster.

Arif sat against the wall and opened his jar of glass marbles. The stock looked woefully depleted. One by one he examined them all. None came close to the beauty of the now-gone white marble.

'Arif, come down, beta.' He heard the fragile voice of his mother calling him downstairs. 'Abba is calling you.'

He packed away the marbles in a small trunk and slid it under his bed before shuffling downstairs, where his father stood combing his henna-coloured greasy hair. His white achkan flaccid on the only chair in the room.

'We are going to the goat market,' Abba said, running the comb through his beard. There was no room for argument in that statement. 'And will you not be as lily-livered as you were last year.'

The creaking pedestal fan nodded to its own rhythm, moving its head between Ammi and Abba as if following the volleys in a tennis match. Arif's cheeks twitched.

'No, ji. Our Arif is a grown man now. But today you go alone, I have some work and I need his help.'

Arif felt a surge of relief and gratitude for his mother. He remembered the goat market last year. Amidst the stench of goat faeces, moist hay, and sweat, he had panicked. Gagging over his own bile, he had walked two paces behind his father trying to avoid the jostling, bleating animals. After what seemed like hours, Abba had stopped in front of a small herd and haggled with a wiry man who spat betel-juice on the road every four minutes. He pinched the thighs, spread the eyes between his thumb and forefinger, inspected horns, hooves and teeth of a white-brown goat before the money changed hands. Arif had walked the sacrificial goat all the way back home and fed her for a week. He had even named her—Reshmi. On the day of Eid al-adha, when the butcher handed him the knife, his fingers had trembled. He couldn't bring himself to place the first slit on the throat of a madly bleating Reshmi. The neighbourhood kids called him Arif the eunuch, and Abba had ever since ignored his existence.

Reshmi is tied to the stump of a tree. Looking at him with one beady eye. Her pupil is white and glazed. A perfect sphere. A swirling hurricane builds inside of it. Gaining momentum. Taking his house and the mosque into its fold. Then it turns red. Liquid. And there's blood everywhere. On his hands and shirt. Over his lips. Even his sweat is blood now.

Arif opens his eyes. He is sure that this wasn't a dream, but it is dark outside and when he looks through the window, there is a young goat nibbling the scant blades of grass in his backyard.

'Bhaijaan, that marble was a gift from my mamu,' he stammered the next evening.

'And?' Basu did not even bother to look at him.

'I have so many other marbles,' he produced a glass jar from his bag. 'You can take any of them. All of them, in fact.'

'Interesting.'

'So, we have a deal? Will you give the white one back to me?' Arif's eyes brightened.

Arif followed Basu around like a wet puppy, waiting for a yes that never came.

Neither did a no. It became his routine, his obsession. All night long he slept restlessly dreaming of slit throats, flailing limbs, and white marbles. He would get up in the middle of the night to check on the animal tied in his backyard. But he never went close to her. Never once fed her. School became a chore. Evenings he would stand in the flanks as other boys played and would then follow Basu around. Pleading.

Entreating. It was only on the fourth day that Arif's tenacity paid off. After roaming around the area for almost half an hour, Basu, stopped under the shade of a banyan and asked, 'Why is it so important to you anyway?'

'It was given to me by my mamu,' came the reply.

'So? Ask him to get you another one,' shot Basu.

'I can't,' Arif said, then added. 'He can't.'

The words sagged in the humid air between the two boys. Basu regarded him for a minute, then said, 'Are you sure you are ready to do anything for it?'

'Absolutely, bhaijaan,' Arif could not believe his luck. 'Whatever you say. Tell me anything?'

'Come with me then,' Basu said and began walking.

Three lanes away, when they reached Basu's house, the door was locked.

Unlocking the main door, Basu took Arif straight to his room, latched the door and reached under his bed. Taped to the bottom of his creaky wooden bed was a copy of *Playboy*. The cover and the centrefold had long been ripped off. The pages were dogeared.

Soiled.

'What is this, bhai?' Arif said. His mouth agape, unable to look away as Basu slowly turned the pages in front of Arif's hungry eyes. Arif hadn't seen anything like that before and the effect was sudden. His soiled grey half-pants bulged up at the fly.

Basu observed the smooth thighs emerging from the khaki half-pants, winked at him and, brushed his fingers lightly at the bulge. He let his hand rest on Arif's thighs for a moment.

'That white marble is nothing man,' he said. 'You can even take this English magazine.' Arif, too shocked to say anything, took a deep breath. He looked at Basu, confused and aroused by the first naked women he had seen in his life.

'It's just a favour,' Basu pushed the magazine into Arif's hands and put an arm around him. 'You get what you want, after I get what I want.'

He opened the magazine to the page where a clean-shaven blonde had spread her legs. The rusted staple, holding the pages together did little to hide her nakedness.

Or willingness. Taking Arif's hand firmly, Basu placed it on his own crotch. It lay there inert. Impatient, he whispered, 'Do it, man, c'mon!'

He arrested Arif's hand and reached inside his pants.

'OK, hold it. Tight. And rub it,' his hand a vice over Arif's fingers. Arif pulled his hand as if stung by a hot iron. Dropping the magazine on the floor, he bolted out of the room. Out of Basu's house. Breathless. His feet pounding the cobblestones. He did not stop until he reached his house and there locked up in his bathroom, scrubbed his hand. Scrubbed till they turned pink and raw. And then exhausted he sat down on the floor and wept.

In the evening, Arif refused dinner. He lay in his bed and kept looking at his hands. Making them into fists, he stuffed them under the pillow and wept into it.

On Sunday, the day of Eid al-adha, the men of the Kazim family, wore their white kurtas and skull caps. The muezzin's call floated down the overhead wires and pooled into Arif's ears. Ammi blew a gentle breath of prayer for success on his forehead and his shoulders. He walked to the mosque, head hung low, eyes boring into his own two feet. At the mosque, he went through the motions with the jamaat. Turning his head to the right and the left, bowing down when he should have, raising his palms in supplication along with everyone else.

Back home, the sacrificial goat was tethered to a pole in the middle of the backyard. A group of men and women—extended family, friends from the neighbourhood, and the butcher—had gathered around for the qurbaani. Men talked and hugged each other three times. Women gossiped. Ammi prayed to an unseen God.

And the goat bleated. Pawed the ground she stood on. Jerked her head, stopping only when the noose around her neck tightened.

'Are you going to do it this time? Or will you chicken out again,' Basu whispered elbowing him from behind. 'Eunuch.'

Arif hadn't noticed him till that moment. He clenched his fists and closed his eyes.

'Anyone from the family would like to halal this animal?' He heard Ishmael, the butcher, call out in his raspy voice and felt the push of his father's palm on his back. He felt the iron-weight of a knife being thrust in his sweaty shaking palm. He sensed his arm being held softly but firmly by the butcher over the throbbing throat of the goat that looked very much like Reshmi. He felt the brown wide eye of the animal burn a hole through his soul. The pupil white and glazed. A perfect sphere. A swirling hurricane building inside of it. Gaining momentum. Then the knife. Slick. Soundless. A thin stream of warm sticky blood ran down Arif's palm.

Much later, Arif would only remember the relief on his mother's face and the glimmer of pride in his father's eyes as he handed the bloodied knife back to the butcher.

NOT A DAY FOR OUTINGS
ARMAAN VERMA

Through the thick haze, Sayma did not see the airborne projectile that smacked her square between the eyes.

When she realized that she had been struck by a rolled-up newspaper, curses came flying out of her mouth at the bitter old goat that came every morning to deliver it on his bicycle. An appropriate response was promptly hurled back. Sayma suspected that his hostility stemmed from the fact that hers was the farthest house to which he pedalled every day, and his old goat hooves would no doubt fall off one day if he continued travelling the distances that he did.

On the outskirts of town, Sayma's house was a doll's house afloat in a sea of garbage. Her great-grandfather had built it with his own hands when it had been in the middle of nowhere, but the chrysanthemums in Sayma's garden now overlooked a rather large slum, which hadn't asked her permission before mushrooming overnight. Despite the filth that bootleggers, immigrants, and industrialists had dumped at her doorstep, she herself kept the house spotless, having inherited it so. She lived with an extensive vase collection and her daughter, Razia. Apart from the occasional stray dog that wandered through her garden, she received no visitors and led a quiet life. If any neighbours asked why she never left the house, she always had a response ready: 'It's not a day for outings today.'

Sayma called out to Razia to join her for an airing as she checked on the state of the flower beds. She had been pointlessly struggling to revive her pitifully weak chrysanthemums, the latest phalanx of flowers that had remained staunchly wilted and failed her. But she loved them nonetheless. Sayma envisioned her flowers shielding her from the corruption and dirt surrounding her—a fortress with petals for ramparts.

She knew that Razia, on the other hand, shared none of her fantasies; for most of the day, her hands clutched a pen and her eyes were trained on a blank page meant for an admissions essay that would perhaps propel her to foreign universities.

'Razia!' Sayma cried out again. This girl would drive her mad one day. She was on strike two.

Sayma stopped in front of her chrysanthemums to examine the poor things once again, a fragile citadel of purity and grace amidst all the filth—a fading benediction.

'Razia!' When the answer was silence, Sayma abruptly stood up. Strike three. That girl has had it. Sayma had been torn from her flowers, a transgression that was reserved only for when the house might be on fire or for the sound of a terrible crash of china from inside it.

Marching into the house, Sayma repeatedly screamed her daughter's name to no avail. She scoured the kitchen, the attic, both bedrooms, both bathrooms, everywhere. When that produced no results, she tore up the floorboards, checked behind paintings for tunnels in the wall, and inspected the piping. It was a matter of pure chance that Sayma was able to spot a strip of paper taped to the tap in the kitchen, containing a message that may well have been written by a mouse's hand, so that one required a

Not a Day for Outings

magnifying glass to read it.

Gone out to look for inspiration. Will be back by five.

Sayma looked at the paper strip, and then at her door, which was letting in a gentle breeze. As she stepped through the door, she began to run. The lanes between the houses had been made slippery with sewage, and her flat shoes bit her feet spitefully at the sudden demands placed upon them. As she made her way through the dreary pathways, people stopped to stare. Even groups of little urchins, who usually troubled all who dared cross their filthy paths, ceased their gambolling and watched as Sayma trundled by. She, in turn, hissed at them. The truth was that most of the neighbourhood had known of a Sayma who had lived in the sanitized doll's house, but its residents had all presumed that she was a witch, disguised as a middle-aged woman. Children had been told before going to bed that her disguise faded away in sunlight but she would come out at night to kidnap anyone and everyone up past their bedtime.

So, naturally, there was much consternation at the witch racing past the homes of the innocent and unsuspecting.

After getting lost twice, Sayma finally arrived at what appeared to be some sort of workshop, though it looked more like a warehouse. She read the sign above the doorless entrance—Devil's Spare Parts.

It looked promising. After all, Razia had always been keen on secretly running out and playing with similarly rustic little creatures as a child. Sayma shivered, remembering the battle of wills, the angry threats, the bedroom doors locked for protection. She had done everything necessary to free her daughter from her frightening intentions, and would do so again a thousand times over.

Upon walking in, Sayma discovered rows of child

labourers wreaking havoc on great twisted masses of machinery with hammers larger than themselves, breaking down the hideous things like furious, miniature Davids. A supervisor sat in a corner, least concerned with the goings-on of the workshop, chewing tobacco while reading a newspaper. 'Idle hands?' Sayma murmured.

'Empty minds, actually,' the supervisor replied, his eyes unmoved from the newspaper.

'I'm looking for my daughter.'

'Is she a motor?'

Sayma blinked. 'No.'

The supervisor grunted in disappointment. The children, soot seeped into their bones, had by now halted all work to gaze in admiration at Sayma's pristine clean dress.

Moving through the slum had left not so much as a speck of mud on it. Scanning the faces of the faceless children, Sayma remained hopeful that Razia would be among them, which would hasten her return to the refuge of her precious vases.

One of the children was bold enough to walk up to her. The little girl pulled out a strip of paper from under her rags. Sayma squinted at it as the girl held it up, cautious to not touch the polluted paper.

I said I'll be back by five!

Silly Razia—always getting lost. She had always been Sayma's little songbird. The poor thing did not understand the dangers of the outside world, the risks of flying carelessly through overcast skies. Sayma left the workshop without another word. The grimy girl watched, her hands a little cleaner now from handling the smooth, white strip of paper.

Sayma was uncertain where to look next. She drifted through the better and worse parts of town as her feet complained louder and louder, sending tidal waves of pain through her body with every step. As she entered a cobbled street, she encountered a prisoner, his hands bound with thick ropes. He was being prodded forward by a constable with a long wooden stake.

Sayma approached the constable and enquired about Razia, but he ignored her. The prisoner looked like the kind of man Sayma would warn Razia about—the reason it was far safer to stay indoors. Nonetheless, she tried her luck with him, beginning by asking him who he was.

'I'm a purveyor of aphrodisiacs myself.'
'Aphrodisiacs?'
'The illegal kind.'
'I'm looking for my daughter.'
'Is she interested in lizard oil?'

This was getting nowhere. The constable seemed to have no qualms about letting his prisoner converse freely with a stranger. He merely stared straight ahead and walked on as if Sayma did not exist. Sayma decided to opt for more aggressive interrogation measures. She slapped the prisoner.

For a moment, even Sayma was shocked. The prisoner narrowed his eyes. 'I saw a group of girls walk into a park east of here,' he snapped. Sayma, having procured an answer that benefitted her, now turned her attention to the constable. She recognized the same deadened intensity in his eyes as she saw in her father while he had been alive.

I know what you're thinking, the prisoner said. He leaned close—until his breath withered her olfactory senses—and whispered, 'It's ganja.'

'Ganja,' Sayma repeated, half-stating and half-asking.
'The illegal kind.' The prisoner grinned.

Sayma took a second look at the constable, standing

painfully upright as if he himself was being prodded by a spear on his behind. His eyes did not comprehend her. She nodded cautiously and backed away as the prisoner burst into unbridled, hysterical laughter. 'The high fool's leading me to my shop!' he cackled.

Sayma turned and ran. She had met far too many weirdos for the day and still no sign of Razia.

The park was not too far away but she effectively increased the distance by moving in a large circle around every piece of garbage lying in her path.

It was one of those Company Gardens from colonial times, fenced off with a black iron gate at the entrance and green enough to make up for the rest of the city. This seems nice, she thought. The park was very much like her own garden, so well-maintained, so disciplined—a barrier against the miasma that sought to contaminate her.

She sat down on one of the benches lining the circular footpath, just to give her feet a moment's rest and breathe in the cool air. The prisoner had said something about swings. She looked around to find a mangled body under a heap of collapsed rubble. She jolted and ran towards it.

It was an adolescent girl whose face she did not recognize. Her lips trembled as she spoke. 'Are you my mother?'

'I'm Razia's mother.'

'That bitch?'

'What?' Sayma was astonished. Did young people always talk such filth? 'Why do you call her a bitch?'

She and some others collapsed this whole swing set on me. 'I don't know if I'll walk again.' The girl began to weep. 'I thought they were my friends—'

'Where is Razia now, child?'

Not a Day for Outings

'They went into the cinema.' She raised a quivering finger. 'Over there.'

Sayma left the girl entangled in splinters and plastic as she dashed through traffic.

The cinema was a square concrete building, as most buildings in the town were. The architects that had planned it only wanted some sort of indoor area where moviegoers could essentially sit, and a square was clearly the most efficient design. The rest of the materials intended for additional washrooms, waiting areas, and a food kiosk had been hauled away to the contractors' homes on wheelbarrows.

This was it. Sayma would finally see her daughter again and be able to bring her home. She entered the cinema hall confidently, knowing that she was in control now. Where her daughter was concerned, she was always in control. The town, that disgusting outside world, now lay behind her. She dusted herself. The crows perched on nearby electric wires watched her intently—they were clearly expecting something (birdfeed?). Sayma, however, had no interest in humouring an audience. She strode into the hall after asking the disinterested schoolboy at the ticket counter what film was being screened. She was almost gone by the time he replied, 'Some Australian one.'

The hall itself reeked of beer (something brewing?). Sayma ignored the big screen and began to scour the seats. It was unnaturally dark for a cinema hall, but then again—when was the last time she had gone for a film? She deliberately walked down the stairs, taking her time to stare down the rows of—men? There were only men in here. Strange.

A gasp resounded through the hall. Only then did Sayma

hear the sounds that chilled her—the moaning of a man and a woman in ecstasy, the sounds of libido that were once so familiar to her. It grew louder, and with every heightened sound the transfixed men leaned forward a little more in their seats. Sayma turned in horror to find skin covering the big screen. She seized the closest man and asked him what film was on. He replied, 'Can't you see?' It's *Tessie Takes a Trip Down Under*.

Sayma instinctively sent up a prayer. Only in the front row did she hear laughter—girls' laughter. She hurried in its direction as she had been doing the entire day and found Razia falling out of her seat laughing.

Sayma began to seethe. Her fists balled up. The whole day's chase had led up to this moment.

It should have been a relief to find her daughter safe and sound but—This!

'Razia! We are going home. Now.' She grabbed the girl by her wrist and began to haul her outside. Razia had by this time caught sight of her mother and had begun to scream, leaving her friends gawking, dumbfounded. The rows upon rows of men turned to find two women struggling against each other while climbing the stairs of the hall.

Razia was cursing her mother without stopping for breath. 'I said I'd be back at five! Why can't you just listen to me?'

'It's not safe.'

'I needed to clear my head. I'm sick of lying at home.'

'You don't have a say in this!'

Finally, Sayma and Razia were out of the cinema. Sayma found the strength to drag Razia on foot all the way back home. On the way she cried out to her daughter, 'How could you hurt that girl in the park?'

'Who, that bitch? She got violent first.'
'See, I'm always telling you it's too dangerous.'
'No! Why can't I take the risk? Why not? Why not? Why *not*?'

So many questions. Sayma ground her teeth—Razia was always asking so many questions.

Why? Why did she have to? It was not as if Sayma did not have her own questions from time to time, but she let them remain just that, never affecting her main flow of thoughts. 'If I say you can't, then you can't,' Sayma said. 'That's it.'

'No, I'm sick of this!'

Sayma's chrysanthemums were in sight. A few moments more and they would be away from this muck, this giant slum that threatened her with its very existence. She finally shoved Razia through the door and shut it. A moment later, she was running out to check on her chrysanthemums. A neighbour, Anand, had been watching the whole affair. He asked Sayma, 'Enjoyed your day out with your daughter?'

'Oh no, it's not at all a day for outings today.'

'But—you just had one, didn't you?'

Sayma stared at Anand, then at the path on which she had returned home. 'Yes...yes, I suppose I have.'

Just as Sayma shut the door behind her, contemplating how beautiful the park had been, how those child labourers had stared at her in wonder, and how boldly Razia had laughed in the cinema hall, she found herself dodging a cooking utensil aimed at her head. Razia roared at her mother. She took a nearby pan and flung it too. Then she began to fling anything handy—forks, knives, mugs, bowls. When Sayma retreated to the living room, Razia flung the television set at her. That one surprised Sayma, who was now terribly afraid. Razia screamed once again. 'I hate you! I hate you with all I've got! You've caged me here like a pet!' Razia proceeded towards the mantelpiece and aimed Sayma's vases at her one by one.

Each vase shattered like a piece of Sayma's heart.

Sayma was numb by now. Her beautiful house! It was being ravaged by her beautiful daughter.

Razia began to spin around holding a chair, destroying anything she could. Tables, drawers, vases, flowerpots, windowpanes—all went up in a whirlwind of debris. But something else had caught Sayma's attention. A smell, like that of when she would leave food in the oven for too long.

Dodging Razia's rampage, Sayma made for the kitchen, half of which she found aflame. Screaming in alarm, she ran for the door, calling for Razia to hurry outside.

The flames spread so quickly! Out of the house, and expecting Razia to be as well, Sayma watched in terror and dismay as the door collapsed in a burning wreckage in a matter of seconds. Soon enough, the attic collapsed as well. Sayma wept and wept in her garden, a mere ten feet from the house her great-grandfather had built, which was now a furious inferno, and hellishly so.

She sat there all night, until all that was left was embers. She lacked the courage to look for Razia's corpse in the seething remains. In the early hours of the morning, when she would have ordinarily begun checking on her chrysanthemums, she now skirted the charred wood. There was a portion of the structure that was half-burnt but had collapsed in a hideous heap.

From there emerged Razia's ashen face, sending Sayma into shock.

Razia cackled and howled and wept, clutching in her

hand a page that was once blank but now crammed with words—the words of Razia's uneventful life, as well as her eventful day out—her soul laid bare on the page. Sayma gasped. Her baby girl! Alive! But Razia was having none of it. Pushing her mother aside, she leapt and skipped with joy, her clothes entirely singed off by the fire. Her naked body, scorched and blistered in places, dashed past Sayma's chrysanthemums, springing into the air, and into the meandering streets of the slum.

Sayma sat there for a long while. Through the morning haze of pollution, a rolled-up newspaper came hurtling towards her, but she caught it in time. She examined it for a moment and threw it right back. Her aim must have been splendid, because it knocked the old goat right off his bicycle and sent him flying into the mud. Sayma shook her head at him as she clambered onto his bicycle, looked at her wilted chrysanthemums for one last time, and set off to find her daughter.

BEATING LONELINESS
JUANITA KAKOTY

Ruksar moved to her mother's house forty years ago when her husband married a second time. They—she and her husband—used to live in a two-room rented apartment above a line of shops in the heart of the teeming Nakhasa Bazaar. The apartment was right on the bend where one found lace and button shops and the husband let go of it when Ruksar packed her bags and left. This happened when the husband married his eldest sister-in-law's first cousin's friend, at the behest of his ailing mother, he said, because Ruksar and his mother never got along, a realization which evidently took twelve years to dawn upon him.

The second wife, everyone knew, came from one of the old wealthy families in Saharanpur who lived in one of the charming havelis at Khambo ka Pul, the haveli most famous for its entrance, where stood a huge wooden door decorated with copper and silver coins. As if that was not enough for all those who had not seen the second wife, her aura was amplified by the fact that she also owned a beautiful house in the outskirts of town, a gift from her grandmother, where Ruksar's husband gladly moved in after the wedding. Tongues wagged in the town about how this kasai, butcher, got lucky. Everyone seemed to forget Ruksar who was wallowing in grief and self-pity. Her predicament compounded when she saw the new bride. Ruksar looked hard at the woman, who she knew was much older than the husband, but what irked her most was that the new bride was not even a match to her below average appearance. This robbed the poignancy of her sadness and gave birth to an eternal hatred for her husband, coming as he did from a family with no assets but consistent good looks and a long history of philandering forefathers. So, Ruksar told the husband to get himself be buggered, and moved in with her mother. He was only too happy to oblige because if the grapevine was to be believed, it was the new bride's eldest brother, the local bodybuilder, who had stolen his sister's thunder.

∽

Ruksar's mother lived in the yellow haveli at the Badtala Yadgar neighbourhood, in its upper storey, with latticed windows overlooking the courtyard, which had been transformed into a thoroughfare with time. In the earlier years, the yellow haveli spread in four directions to enclose this courtyard, where in a corner lay the Sufi saint Shah Harun Chisti's shrine and a huge banyan tree. The owners of the glorious haveli had shifted to Lahore at the time of the Partition in 1947 and a few refugee families from Pakistan were given ownership to parts of this haveli by the Indian government. Ruksar's mother acquired a portion of this haveli, consisting of three rooms, when, many years later, in search of greener pastures, the refugee-owners left for Delhi and other places. The insides of the haveli were in tatters by then and three of its wings had already fallen. Only three rooms stood, floating in the ruins. This became home for the two women.

It is interesting how Ruksar's mother, Inayat Begum,

had moved into the yellow haveli. She was in her mid-twenties, widowed and abandoned by her in-laws as well as her maternal relatives. She had married a homeopath who fought with his family to stray from the family tradition of doing nothing but living off the huge acres of mango orchards, where bonded labours toiled night and day. The tragedy of her life was that she could bear only one child, that too a girl, after many years of consuming the roots and leaves and juices of this and that. This did not go down well with her in-laws who harped on the merits of several children to carry the lineage forward. When Ruksar turned five years old and Inayat Begum produced no more progeny, especially a male child, her in-laws let not even a month pass before throwing her and the child out when the homeopath died of sudden cardiac arrest.

Inayat Begum first went to her mother's home, the dark green Hari kothi, not quite a haveli but the miniature replica of a haveli that her grandfather had built. The kothi housed about thirty people in all and was right at the mouth of Nakhasa Bazaar when one approached it from Nehru market. Inayat Begum lived there for a few months but when the taunts of her five sisters-in-law became too much to bear, she moved with little Ruksar to the yellow haveli in the early 1950s. She sold all of her gold jewellery to obtain this piece of shelter. It was here that Ruksar, later on, raised her three bright boys and one daughter who heaped great ignominy upon her by fleeing with a Hindu lad in her teens.

The crumbling yellow haveli witnessed how Inayat Begum struggled with her daughter to build their lives from scratch. The older woman bought a sewing machine on loan and took to stitching ladies' salwar kameez. By the time Ruksar had turned fourteen, she became an expert at it too.

But people love to talk, whether be it in villages, towns, or cities. And they talked about Inayat Begum and Ruksar as cursed women. People had their own reasons to believe this even when they had no clue about their own lives. So it wasn't funny when Mariam Bibi, whose daughters-in-law just couldn't stand her and escaped to their maternal homes every now and then, spoke of these two women as accursed. Nor was it funny when Bilal dhobi spoke of them as cursed even when all that he had done with his life was to waste it on opium!

The forty-year-old Maulana's son, who was a father to nine children and yet to earn his first morsel, spoke of them as cursed too. He, in fact, tried to drill wisdom in other men by elaborately articulating why not to choose women with foreheads and gait like Inayat Begum and Ruksar as wives.

Ruksar was only sixteen when she fell in love with the kasai's son from whom her mother bought meat. As Inayat Begum and the old kasai exchanged instructions, meat, and money, Ruksar and the young kasai, who assisted his father in that little shop from where hung the white meat of skinned goats, locked eyes as the world passed by in cycle rickshaws and motorbikes. Since Inayat Begum would never agree to her daughter marrying a kasai, Ruksar eloped with the young man, produced four children back-to-back without ever meeting her mother. It was only when she realized that love didn't last forever and, more crucially, because she had nowhere to go, that she stepped into the yellow haveli again. This time with her four little children. A much older Inayat Begum merely looked at all of them and went about her routine as if she had seen them every day of her life.

Now almost seventy, Ruksar lived in the yellow haveli with the nearly paralysed Inayat Begum, who prayed to the Lord every day to take her away. When her daughter eloped, Ruksar came to assume a stoic presence around the house and acted as if she was the caretaker of an inn since the sons never gave as much as the daughter did to the home. She didn't complain about it but she did miss her daughter. All her life she had woven dreams for her sons: salaried jobs and dutiful daughters-in-law who would produce charming kids and slog in the house while their husbands earned money in offices. She hardly thought of her daughter's future, although it was the daughter who took care of the whole house along with her. But destiny had other plans. The three sons went on to scale brilliant careers, but none stayed back in Saharanpur.

The eldest went to Bombay where he started writing scripts for television serials. He made good money, sent a substantial amount home, which is why Ruksar did not protest when he married a Marathi girl, who also had a media job and earned well. That her granddaughters spoke in Marathi saddened her to the core, but she did not say a word beyond a meek 'you should talk to them in Hindi' to her daughter-in-law and kept quiet when the young woman smiled and said, 'Inshallah, they will learn Hindi anyway, everybody in India does.' The second son got a job as an assistant professor at Delhi University and found himself a lawyer wife born and brought up in Delhi. Ruksar was quite pleased with this match because the girl was from a prestigious Mughal family in Old Delhi. But when they chose not to have a child, Ruksar did not quite understand the why of it. She all the more didn't understand why they allowed a dog inside the house, didn't refer to it as a 'dog', and took care of it like their son. The third son, her favourite, moved to the United Kingdom on a scholarship, where he married a British woman and stayed there for the rest of his life. For a long time, Ruksar engaged in tactics to somehow convert the British daughter-in-law to Islam. This did not happen primarily because the daughter-in-law visited Saharanpur only about twice in her life, and because Ruksar never visited the United Kingdom, although the son came once in every two–three years, and stayed for at least a month. When they had a son as fair and pink as the mother, Ruksar's health received a jolt because she was sure he would grow up as a Christian.

∽

A few days to her seventieth birthday, Ruksar started complaining of severe knee pain. A visit to the doctor revealed that she was flat-footed as well. That day, she was on her way to the oldest shoemaker in town to order a pair of sandals for herself, fit for her flat feet, when she saw streams of coloured paper and tiny plastic bulbs hanging above the narrow street, strung from the buildings on either side, right where Hari kothi was.

Her heart skipped a beat. What's happening here, she thought, nobody told me anything.

Forgetting about the new sandals, she quickly darted inside Hari kothi, her mother's maternal home, which was still as glorious inside, never mind the rush, dirt, vehicles, and garbage that the street outside had collected over the years.

'Asalaamaleikum!' She uttered just as she stepped into the courtyard and saw two of her surviving aunts, old and wrinkled and crinkled, sitting on a charpoy in the veranda where the ceiling was held up by three white round pillars.

A maid was sweeping the courtyard with a short broom that was tied to a long wooden handle.

The aunts looked at her and thought a beggar had just walked in.

'It's me,' Ruksar offered, moving toward the charpoy, 'Inayat Begum's daughter.'

The aunts squinted and looked hard at her. 'Oh,' they said in their quivering voices, not quite sounding excited.

'Where is everybody?' Ruksar asked.

'Oh them,' an aunt responded, as the other one leisurely extended her shaky hand toward the heavy silver paandaan, now blackened with time, and made herself a paan. 'They are at the neighbour's, attending a wedding.'

Ruksar felt relieved. Had something been happening at Hari kothi and no one informed her, she would have been insulted, like the several times before when she got to know that some function had happened at Hari kothi and she, her children, and her mother were not invited. All that changed once her boys became achievers. She became a permanent feature at every function that took place at Hari kothi. So that day, the sight of the streamers and tiny plastic bulbs hanging in the air outside the street stirred the familiar old humiliation in her.

'But as far as I remember, your neighbours have no more children to be married off,' Ruksar pondered aloud.

The aunt whose mouth was filled with an enormous paan spoke this time. 'It ish the shecond marriaghe of one of their shonsh, the one who shtaysh in Zhaipur and hash no shildren. Shomezhing wrong wizh hish wife, hish mozher shaysh. Sho she ish geshing him anozher wife who will shtay wizh her here in Shaharanpur while zhe will conzhinue to live wizh hish firsht wife in Zhaipur.'

Beating Loneliness

Ruksar's mind raced at this possibility. 'What about the kids he would have through his second marriage?'

'Zhe mozher shaysh she will keep the shecond wife and kidsh from her here in Shaharanpur.'

Ruksar was hit by a eureka moment! The aunt was still saying something, but she didn't hear a single word. Her mind was fast calculating which of her sons would be best for a second marriage. After all, she needed someone in the house to talk to, someone who made her feel alive, unlike her paralysed mother who was as good as the furniture in the house. On her way back home, she decided that the sons in India would not be appropriate for her cause; the youngest one with the British wife who hardly came to Saharanpur would be the ideal candidate.

So that Eid, she called her two sons in India home. And they came with their families. It was a long time since all of them had gathered together, at least the ones in India. Ruksar informed them about her plans for the youngest son. Speak to him, they suggested. But Ruksar admitted she didn't have the courage and requested one of them to do it. No one took up the responsibility. That Eid went by with yakhni pulao, sewaiyya, and kebabs, without any further mention of the second marriage.

A few days later, the Marathi daughter-in-law called to say, 'It's a very bad plan, Ammi. I don't know about you, but I would feel very bad if my husband married a second time.'

This daughter-in-law did know about Ruksar's husband's second marriage years ago. So, the old lady kept quiet, but that didn't deter her spirit. She waited for the time when her youngest son would come home. And when he finally did, without his wife or kid, Ruksar grabbed the opportunity.

'Just two–three kids for positive energy in the house,' she told him, 'and nothing has to change between you and your family in the UK. In fact, you can continue to come once every two years. I'll look after your family here.' The son bought that. After all, as Ruksar always said, this son was more of a friend who understood the pathos of her life.

That very visit, the son got married to a pale, sickly girl from an impoverished family, who was a good twenty years younger than him. This was a match recommended by Ruksar's cousin who lived in Roorkee. Apparently, the girl's family was desperately looking to get her hitched so they had one mouth less to feed. Ruksar immediately liked her because the cousin specifically said, she has downcast eyes and the decency not to talk back to elders and has the experience of bringing up seven siblings. Like these were the assets that mattered most for a woman to be eligible as a daughter-in-law.

There was no function held to announce the wedding. The son had particularly advised so. No invitation was sent out either. And after he left, the girl swept and mopped the house, cooked food, washed the clothes and dishes and looked after both Ruksar and the paralysed Inayat Begum, who anyway had no idea what was happening. Ruksar had told her that this pale girl was a daughter-in-law but Inayat Begum registered nothing.

Two months later, the girl vomited in the morning. A home kit confirmed her pregnancy and a happy Ruksar called up her sons in India to convey the good news. Nobody was as thrilled about it as her, and her youngest son especially asked all not to ever mention this woman or her pregnancy to his British wife. But Ruksar was so happy that she distributed sweets to the poor and went all the way to the Kaliyar

Sharif dargah to offer a chadar. She got almonds and desi ghee ladoos for the girl and made her have a huge glass of milk with saffron in the mornings. But she did not stop the girl from doing the housework.

Thus the days went by with the girl growing heavier. But there came a day when Ruksar passed away in her sleep looking extremely peaceful. The girl stood at the doorway, holding her bulging belly tenderly in both hands, feeling desperate. She went and whispered to Inayat Begum that her daughter was no more. The old woman, senile with age, looked at her and said, 'Shoo! Go away! Who let you in?'

She left the old woman in her dark room, where all day just a peep of the sun was allowed in through a crack in the window and dragged herself to the Hari kothi, where residents called up the sons to convey news of the demise. Everyone came. The last rites were conducted. But nobody came from the United Kingdom. In fact, the youngest son never ever came to Saharanpur again. Soon there were talks among the brothers that the apartment be sold off, when Inayat Begum dies, which would be soon considering the state she was in, and the girl be given some money and sent back to her family. The season had not yet turned when Inayat Begum's heart stopped beating. A few days later, the yellow haveli with latticed windows bid adieu to its last inhabitant and began to resemble an old lonely woman who has outlived all her family members.

SAVED BY THE TERRORISTS

RANJAN PAL

Shivani awoke with a start as the library clock chimed eleven times with dull, reverberating tones. She looked blurrily around as the unfamiliar outlines of the large room swam before her. Then as her vision cleared, she realized where she was. And why. In the Ratan Tata Memorial Reading Room at the Delhi School of Economics. Doing some last-minute cramming to pass that wretched Applied Econometrics exam tomorrow. She cursed the day that she had signed up for this 'killer' option in a fit of bravado. As the term ground on, others in the course dropped like flies. But Shivani had persevered because she had not yet learned how to give up gracefully. It was one of her most admirable traits—but it could also create trouble for her.

Shivani knew all this, of course. Her family knew it, her friends knew it—and now Kartik, her latest romantic entanglement, knew it. She wondered where their relationship was headed. They had only known each other for a few weeks and, at first, they had hit it off surprisingly well. They had met at the PVR multiplex when both had gone to see *Bridget Jones' Diary*. They knew each other vaguely from D School and had come with separate sets of friends. After the movie, the whole gang had unanimously decided that a few drinks at TGIF were in order. One thing had led to another and now they were a couple. Shivani smiled at

Saved by the Terrorists

the memory and the irony of meeting someone new in her life, right after a comedy chronicling the romantic problems of a single girl.

Kartik had said that he would come by eleven and pick her up from the RTL. It was no longer safe to walk the Delhi U campus alone at night. Just a week ago a girl had disappeared from the Jubilee Hall women's hostel. The warden had informed her parents who lived in a distant district town but they hadn't heard from her. There was a rumour that she had been suffering from depression and had tried to commit suicide. Others said that she was part of a college call girl ring and was frequently seen in the company of strange men. The truth was that no one really knew what had happened to her. It just gave one an uneasy feeling.

Wearily, Shivani gathered the shiny red copy of Kmenta's *Elements of Econometrics* that had slid to the floor and her lecture notes and struggled to her feet. The room was empty except for a couple of Socio types, poring over their books. She stepped out of the musty library and was instantly invigorated by the nip in the night air. Shivani took a deep breath and looked around for Kartik. But there was no one to be seen except for an old chowkidar, huddled under the flickering streetlamp.

The stillness of the night unnerved her. It was unlike Kartik to be so late, especially when he knew that she would be all alone and waiting for him. She decided she'd give him five more minutes and looked at her watch. The green dial of the Swatch Irony glowed in the dark: 11:18, Tue, Sept. 11. The minutes ticked by as Shivani walked up and down, trying to keep warm. Finally, she decided that he wasn't coming. She hoped the buses were still running as she walked quickly towards the entrance.

The bus stop was just around the corner, impossible to detect in the fog and the darkness. There was not a soul in sight. As Shivani stood undecided and nervous, wondering what to do, a voice spoke suddenly from behind her, making her jump in fright.

'Looks like it's going to be a long wait.' Shivani whirled around and saw the shrouded figure huddled in the corner of the shelter. A cigarette glowed in his cupped hand. All she could see of his face was the fiery reflection in a pair of intense, dark eyes that seemed to look straight through her. Shivani looked away, fighting down the urge to turn and run. What to do now? Why hadn't she just waited for Kartik a little longer?

The figure spoke again in a deep, rough voice. 'Why do you look so scared, pretty one?' and began to edge closer to her. A surge of panic began to well up inside her and she looked around wildly for help. There was still no one in sight. Just as she had made up her mind to run, the sound of hurrying feet caused her to whirl around, dropping the Kmenta. To her huge relief, the figure of Kartik materialized out of the gloom, running as if the very Devil was after him. He skidded to a stop in front Shivani, his breath coming in huge, ragged gulps. The shrouded figure had melted away into the darkness.

'Where have you been? Why the hell are you so late?' she cried out, grabbing him by the lapels and shaking him urgently.

'Some...something terrible has happ...happened!' he spluttered, fighting to get his breath back.

'What...WHAT has happened!?' Shivani demanded, fighting down the urge to scream. Kartik grabbed her by the wrist and began to pull her in the direction from which he had come.

'It's...it's...It's just...just unbelievable! You have to...to see it...for...yourself!' Kartik was making no sense at all but Shivani decided to conserve her breath as she half-walked half-ran along with him. She had never seen him so shaken.

In a few minutes, they had reached the women's hostel and Shivani immediately realized that something was amiss. Normally the courtyard would have been deserted at this time of night. Now she could see a small crowd spilling out of the Common Room whose lights blazed into the night. Kartik pulled her along behind him as he pushed his way through the silent throng, their eyes glued to something at the front of the room. Filled with growing dread, Shivani thrust herself forward until she could see what they were staring at.

She too fell silent, stunned by the spectacle unfolding on the TV screen. Before her lay the expanse of lower Manhattan stretching away into the distance, crowned by the imposing, tall spires of the World Trade Centre. But something was horribly wrong with the picture. A huge, thick plume of black smoke engulfed the crown of the North Tower, darkening the clear blue sky above. The film was being shot from a high floor somewhere in midtown. Shivani could hear the excited voice of the CNN anchor as he described how a plane had flown directly into the tower. Could it be just a horrible accident? Or something else?

And then she saw it, a tiny speck streaking across the screen from left to right, seemingly disappearing behind the South Tower. Before her mind had time to register what the speck was, a huge ball of fire and smoke erupted from the middle of the tower. For a moment, Shivani had the surreal feeling of watching a particularly bad disaster movie. Maybe this was just Armageddon II. Then reality returned with a crash. The Common Room had fallen deathly silent as its occupants grappled with the enormity of what they had just seen. The CNN commentary had been cut off in mid-flow; only the searing images remained. Months later, Shivani would remember this shattering moment when time itself appeared to have stopped.

The rest of the evening passed in a blur. The mortally wounded towers crumbled and fell to the earth in great clouds of dust. CNN reported that two more planes had crashed, one of them into the Pentagon. Was the world coming to an end? Students stumbled out of the Common Room to call their friends and relatives in the US. Some girls sobbed quietly in a corner, their faces buried in their hands. Others clustered in shocked knots to discuss and speculate as to who was behind this devastating act of terrorism. And why?

So much destruction, so many innocent lives snuffed out. How could this possibly be justified?

Shivani sat with her back to the wall, numbly watching the movie from hell unfold on the TV screen, Kartik's arm around her. She glanced at the Swatch and was startled by the time—2:15 a.m.! Time had slipped by, unnoticed. She had better get to bed. That damn Trics paper was tomorrow. No chance of it being postponed because of what had happened, she thought wryly. No, that would only happen if a plane flew into the D School building itself.

Shivani stood up and stretched. A wave of weariness washed through her. She could barely keep her eyes open. Kartik also made as if to get to his feet but Shivani stopped him. She told him that she was going to bed and after kissing him a little self-consciously, she turned and left. The cold night air hit her as she emerged from the warmth of the Common Room. She shivered and wrapped her shawl tighter around her. Turning, she headed down the unlit corridor. Coming to a flight of steps, she clambered through the darkness to the second floor. The room she shared with Kavita was the last one on the left.

Kavita. Shivani hoped that her roommate would be asleep. She was in no mood to discuss the traumatic events of the night with her. She would only bombard Shivani with all sorts of inane questions. Shivani sighed inwardly. It would have been difficult to find two more unlikely roommates. Shivani's close friend and confidante, Ayesha, had had to leave in the middle of term because of a family tragedy. And so Shivani inherited Kavita as a replacement roommate.

Kavita was attractive in an obvious sort of way. She came from a middle-class business family and was marking time before her family found her a suitable boy to get married to. She was studying for her Masters in Psychology but found the attractions outside class more compelling. On more than one occasion, Shivani had come back to the room to find Kavita locked inside with one of her male admirers. When Shivani pointed out that this was against the rules, Kavita merely replied with a lascivious wink that Shivani should try it sometime. As a result, Shivani spent as little time as possible in the room, only using it to change and to sleep.

Now she fumbled with her key in the lock until the door opened with a loud click. Shivani held her breath, hoping that the noise had not awoken Kavita, and stepped into the room. She shivered in the cold draft from the window that overlooked the lawn at the back. Kavita must have left it open—really she was so irresponsible. The fire escape could easily be accessed from the window which should have given Shivani a feeling of security but didn't. She crossed the room and shut it quietly.

Standing in the darkness, she debated whether to turn on the light and get changed. Her exhaustion got the better of her and she stumbled to her side of the room and collapsed onto her bed. As her eyes got accustomed to the light, Shivani thought the dark mound on Kavita's bed was too large to be just one person. Had her roommate brought a male friend home for the night? It would be just like her to take that risk. She thought of jumping out of bed, turning on the light and screaming at her. But she was just too tired to bother...just too...tired...and soon she slipped into a deep, comforting slumber.

The scream echoed through the corridors of Jubilee Hall as the sky lightened above its spires. It awoke Mrs Paintal, the hostel warden, instantly from a deep sleep. Fumbling for her specs, she hurriedly threw on a shawl and ran out into the corridor. The scream went on and on and on, terrifying in its intensity, making her hair stand on end. She stumbled towards the source of the noise, her cotton nightgown flapping behind her. A small bunch of girls had collected outside Kavita and Shivani's room. Some of them banged on the door but it was locked on the inside. Mrs Paintal shoved her way to the front and ordered the girls to stand back. She shouted at the two security guards, who had just come up to see what all the fuss was about, to break down the door. The guards rammed their shoulders against the door, which refused to give. All the time, the horrible screaming hadn't stopped.

Finally, the old wooden frame splintered under the repeated battering and the door collapsed with a crash.

Ordering the guards to hold the crowd back, Mrs Paintal rushed into the room. Shivani sat huddled on her bed, her knees drawn tightly up under her. She was screaming hysterically, her body shaking like a leaf, her mouth wide open as she pointed at something across the room. Mrs Paintal swivelled and gasped in shock. Kavita's half-naked body lay sprawled across the bed. She had been stabbed savagely and repeatedly. The blood from several wounds had soaked into the bedclothes and the mattress. Her once-pretty face was frozen in the rictus of death, eyes starting from their sockets.

The warden glanced back at Shivani. Her terrified eyes stared blindly at the opposite wall, her outstretched arm trembling like a tree branch in a storm. And then Mrs Paintal realized that she wasn't pointing at the body but at something above it. She raised her eyes and then she saw it. Something straight out of a nightmare. Even though the words had been scrawled in an uneven hand, they were clearly legible. 'Aren't you glad you didn't turn on the lights?' The blood had run from the bottom of the Y's and G's and pooled on the floor.

∽

Days later, Shivani lay in bed at her parent's home in Vasant Vihar, groggy from the sedatives. The police had questioned her and then let her leave the hostel to recover from her shock. Everyone had been very kind and understanding. Kartik had helped her pack and escorted her home. The university authorities had agreed to let her reschedule her exams. But Shivani's mind was in turmoil, like a tape stuck on constant rewind. The police had established the time of Kavita's death as occurring sometime between 11.30 and 12 midnight. The very time that Shivani would have returned to her room. And run straight into the killer. Had it not been for two planes that had crashed into two buildings she had never seen. Had it not been for the worst terrorist attacks the world had ever known. Thousands she would never know had died in those attacks. But she was alive... saved by the terrorists.

LATA AND THE MERMAID

C. JAYANTI

Seated in a corner of the room, her legs primly folded, in her beige slacks and peach top with its long flouncy sleeves, a glass of non-alcoholic fruit punch in her hand, its rim stamped by her mauve lips, nervously fluttering her peach-dusted eyelids, why did Lata suddenly find herself on the verge of tears at Leo Fernandes' fiftieth birthday party? All around her there was laughter and applause, people were singing along and eating and drinking, trying their best to have a cheerful evening, to make the best of this modest celebration and, to all appearances, succeeding, yet what secret inner calamity had befallen Lata?

Nothing in front, nothing at the back. That's what the girls in college would say about her. Scarecrow, lamp post— these were some of the names her body had earned her in school. In tuition classes, she'd heard the boys whisper behind her back—carrom board. She was plain old Lata, stick thin, gaunt as a cadaver, fleshless. Skin, like wrapping paper, tied tightly around her bones. X-Ray—another of her nicknames. Growing up, she'd shrugged off the filings of nastiness she drew towards her like a long, slender magnetic rod, focused on academics. Good thing she's good at her lessons, her grandmother had said in that shrewd, cold-blooded voice of hers, opening the lid of her dainty tin and leisurely and luxuriantly inhaling the pinch of snuff she tucked into her nostril with all the affection with which one would place a treat in the mouth of a beloved pet. She'll have to be independent.

Well, Lata hadn't done too badly for herself. She'd graduated with a first class in commerce, went on to work as an office assistant. She was now employed with a multinational company as assistant manager, admin. She was supervisor to a squad of pantry staff and office boys, forever irate, recalcitrant, and unreliable. They, too, probably had names for her; she was certain that she was now the butt of a whole new set of jokes. But it did not bother her; she focused on her job, on fulfilling her responsibilities and getting others to perform their own.

Madam, you are very kadak, one of the cleaning ladies told her one day, a blunt forty-something mother of three, whose favoured choice of clothing was gaudy saris (so that one was shocked if one caught sight of her after she'd changed out of her drab uniform at the end of her shift) and who perpetually arrived late to work. Madam, I have to get up early, get my kids ready, prepare breakfast, and then tiffin for all of us. After that I have to fill the water, do little cleaning—whatever is possible here and there—and then rush to get ready for work. It's not easy, taking care of the entire household, catering to each family member's whims and fancies...you know how children can be...and here she trailed off, averting her eyes, a cunning look in them. Lata became the epitome of the epithet the woman had labelled her with. She felt an angry shiver down her spine, her arm trembled. In a steely voice, she said, 'Please try and get up earlier. I have heard enough of your stories.'

They came, they went. They carped, they lied. She knew their tricks and excuses.

Lata and the Mermaid

I could write a book about dealing with these people, she often thought to herself on her train journeys, flicking through her phone or absently staring out the window. To her, they seemed lazy, weak willed. Most of them anyway. What they needed was to be determined, disciplined. And this is where she saw herself coming in. She did, however, believe in giving credit where credit was due, was generous with increments and bonuses towards those she found genuinely deserving. Yet she knew that this only made tongues wag about how she was partial, how so-and-so had been rewarded only for flattering their boss and always smooching her non-existent backside. People will talk, you can't please everyone, Lata told herself. As a boss, it was only natural that she be reviled and hated. She went on her rounds, notepad in hand, always sensibly dressed, wearing matching and subtle make-up and carrying herself very erectly.

'Joshi, I had asked you to stack up the tissue boxes neatly on this side of the storeroom. Still it is not done. And have you done the count of the liquid soap packets delivered in the morning?'

'Madam, I was just finishing some tea orders.'

'Why, where is Santosh?'

'He has gone downstairs to serve tea to the guards.'

'It is now fifteen minutes past ten o'clock. Till now what was he doing?'

'Lata madam, it is a question you must pose to him.' And he walked away without even turning to look at her.

She scribbled something on the notepad and moved to the kitchen area. The woman inside was hiding behind the wall. Lata was well acquainted with her work-shirking tactics. A tower of dishes leaned precipitously against the edge of the wash basin.

When Lata confronted her later, she would say she was on an urgent phone call, her baby or mother or a visiting relative was not keeping well. Illness was constantly at her door, a persistent salesman offering irresistible deals. She committed a few more words to her page. She would raise the matter with her own boss, head of admin. He always had so many things on his mind, a hundred matters to attend to, it was difficult to get hold of him. But their weekly meeting was only two days away. She would save these issues for then.

Leo Fernandes was infamous for his short temper. Not a whimper of dissent escaped the mouths of these louts when he questioned them. They hung their heads in embarrassment, hands behind their backs, uttering monosyllables only when absolutely required to, and otherwise silently soaking up his tirades. There was none of the impudence that she was dished out. Where did all their smartness go when they were faced with the wrath of Leo sir? she asked herself as she combed and tied her long, nearly waist-length hair in front of the mirror, or pouted and rubbed together her freshly coloured lips.

It was only because she was who she was, ugly, unremarkable, skeletal Lata, a spinster in her early thirties, that they treated her the way they did. With such an utter lack of respect. So, well, lightly.

In any case, at least she had more control over the circumstances of her life, she thought, slipping on her earphones and tuning into her favourite radio station, the one that played soulful music from black-and-white Bollywood films (from another era, an era so different from the loud and crass and unscrupulous one she was unfortunate to belong to and live in). She had taken charge of them, had refused to be a victim. She was confident, she was hardworking. And she did not give a damn about what they said about her.

And yet if she was strong, if she was all those things she claimed to be, why had she almost burst into tears at her boss's birthday party, a surprise party his wife had organized and invited some close family friends and a few of his office colleagues?

5

The boy was sitting on a stool in the centre of the room. He was around nineteen or twenty, long-haired and lanky, a quiet and serious-looking type. The guests were urging him to sing another song: 'Come on, men, Lenny! One more, one more!'

He'd played Happy Birthday and then, on popular demand, a brief medley of party staples and now it looked like he couldn't wait to escape from the room. He got up and then someone tried to push him back down on the stool and then that person was distracted by someone or something and the boy just remained like that, with the lower half of his body bent in an about-to-sit-down/get-up posture above the stool, the acoustic guitar slung around his shoulder.

Then a man shouted from across the room, 'Eh, Lenny, where do you think you're going?' and he sat down again sheepishly, adjusting the concave waist of the guitar on his thigh and pushing some of his long hair out of his face.

My Bonnie lies over the ocean...
O bring back, O bring back,
O bring back my Bonnie to me...to me...
You are my sunshine,
My only sunshine...you'll never know dear,
how much I love you...

Stupid songs, silly songs. And there was nothing exceptional about the way the boy sang or played. Which was not to say he was bad or not talented. But why why why had the performance stirred up such a whirlwind of emotions in Lata's heart? She wanted to cry. She said excuse me to the broad and oldish lady who was seated next to her, who turned and smiled vaguely and then continued jabbering to her companion, and then went in the direction of the kitchen from where Leo sir's wife kept appearing with trays of food.

She lingered there in the doorway. Inside, Mrs Fernandes was meticulously loading up a plate of canapés topped with some cheesy-looking mixture. She was saying to a slim fashionably dressed middle-aged woman beside her, 'Shirley, just like you said, I went easy with the...' and then she looked up and broke off her sentence and said, 'Oh, hi Lata, Mr Tiwari hasn't arrived yet, you must be feeling lost among the guests, and I'm so sorry, I've been caught up with all the preparations, I haven't had the chance to sit down and chat...'

Earlier that evening, when she was serving chicken croquettes, Lata had hesitated and Mrs Fernandes exclaimed, rather too loudly, 'Gosh, you of all people making a fuss! Come now, eat up. Take two, not one.' And she promptly slid two pieces onto Lata's plate as Lata smiled awkwardly. She smiled again now and nodded. She'd dabbed at her eyes with her handkerchief but from the way Mrs Fernandes regarded her she knew she still looked the picture of unhappiness, so she stood up straight and said, 'That's all right. No worries. But I wanted to ask you, where is the washroom?'

In the washroom, she splashed water on her face, not caring that she was ruining her make-up. She cursed when she wet the edges of her dangling sleeves. She could still hear the singing from the living room but she did not pay attention. She had her dinner, mildly irritated by her damp sleeves, nibbled on the tasty food, exchanged a few words with Pawar and Tiwari and then thanked her hosts and left.

'Lata dear, hope you enjoyed yourself,' said Mrs Fernandes at the door. 'Leo is busy yakking away with someone...The gift you all gave...the ties and the cuff links... it was very thoughtful...thank you so much. Good night, girl. Take care.'

When the rickshaw was just half a kilometre from her home, she suddenly announced that she wanted to be taken to the beach.

The driver made no comment and dropped his passenger off at the new destination. It was half-past eleven but there was still quite a crowd. Families with little children and romancing couples. She passed a tacky plaster statue of a mermaid they had recently installed on the beach. The mermaid had a wistful look in her eyes. The reason for her distress, Lata surmised, was twofold: (a) she wasn't supposed to exist, (b) but now that she did, she was condemned to a life of desolation on this high plinth, outside of her habitat. The scales of her tail and her seashell-shaped bikini top were a glittering green. A crown of orange and red and yellow flowers sat heavy and lopsided on her head. She was voluptuous but not very pretty. Most importantly, she was hollow. In a picture book someone had given to her as a child or that she'd borrowed from the school library, she remembered one of the illustrations of the mermaid from the tragic fairy tale, biped and aching and betrayed, standing by the marital bed of her handsome and stupid prince and his gorgeous bride, clutching in her hands the knife her sisters had procured from the witch of the deep by shaving their long blonde hair. There the knife hung, tensely in the charged air. Would she, wouldn't she? For a moment, Lata was seized by an urgent desire to pick up a rock and smash the mermaid's skull. She turned rigid and then she shook violently but not too discernibly. No one looked at her except a man selling plastic-wrapped fluffy bales of cotton candy. She hoped she would not attract any pests. She trudged through the sand and then down to the pitch black water. She took off her one-inch block-heeled sandals that were making her feet ache. Holding them by the straps, she stood at the edge of the water and wet her feet. A man with a camera and an album of pictures with customers smiling and flashing the peace sign came up to her and asked her if she would like a photograph. She flirted with the idea of striking coquettish Madhubalaesque poses by the seaside. But she was no nymph, no siren. She said a brusque no and exited the water.

Haal kaisa hai janaab ka....?

The lyrics of a vintage Bollywood song.

At least if she were manglik *or something, there was something we could do for her...ward off the negative influence by marrying her to a peepul tree...but as it is...*

Her snuff-addicted grandmother's words again.

But as it is, Lata said to herself, I'm just doomed to be loveless, to be alone.

Her father called. She said she was on her way. She hurried back to the road. A man in a torn T-shirt and loose shorts said, 'Hi, baby, are you lonely?' There was an unfocused look in his eyes and he was swaying on his feet. A gang of burly sari-clad eunuchs went cackling by and one of them said, 'Eh, Pedro, stop harassing decent people. Coming with me or what?'

Lata and the Mermaid

Lata got into a parked rickshaw, gave the driver her address.

A few months ago, a decent-looking chap had moved into their neighbourhood and she told herself there was no need to be desperate and not to get her hopes too up, but despite that she went out of her way to smile at him, dressed to catch his eye and impress him, only to discover that he was engaged. As for her grandmother, years of nicotine intake had addled her brain. That was all she would say.

But everything was sad and hopeless! The stars were angels' fallen teardrops, glowing upon the black glass of the sky. Bemoaning our fate, the terrible hell we had made of our beautiful world after our fall....

What fall? And what Bonnie? What sunshine?

She was an idiot, as big an idiot, undoubtedly, as the mythical *little* creature of the story. But certainly not the only one. Just the other day she'd read in the papers about a woman who claimed to be married to a railway station. The station talked to her, apparently, and promised to love her forever. They had even consummated their relationship. How exactly did they make love? The rumbling of trains through the station made the lady's sex shudder, was it? Or did touching a certain wall send a frisson of sensual delight rippling through her privates? She did not recall the details. In any case, here she was, wanting to crack open the head of a pathetic statue of a mermaid...Something else then? More worthy of her feelings and devotion? A BEST bus depot? The statue of an imperious prince? Or perhaps a fiery politician? A painting maybe? Or her grandmother's snuff box even? A peepul tree then? She could give it a shot, regardless of what the stars and planets had to say. Or would a banyan make a more long-lasting companion?

There was a bewildering variety of options when one thought about it. But, she realized, she did not want to. She paid the fare, got off the rickshaw, and wearily climbed up the stairs to her flat, each step cutting through her feet like a hundred sharp knives.

THE ANKLET ON HER LEFT FOOT

IPSITA MISHRA

'...She kept me warm in this unforgiving cold.'
She opened her bleary eyes when the cat, all seven pounds of squirming flesh, climbed onto her belly. Squinting into the sunlight streaming in from the open window, she discovered that she was now the possessor of a pounding headache, and at some point, had managed to lose both a tooth and a spouse.

The words were ringing in her ears.

It had been ten years since life had moved on for Sanjukta but the memory of that cruel winter weekend haunted her every season without any warning, or apology. She woke up with a jerk. Her cat, after catching a few winks on her belly, had stealthily made its way into the kitchen. Summer months in Delhi were harrowing. Sanjukta was alone. The sky outside her window wore a hue that transported her to an unforgiving winter evening, few forgotten years ago. Everything seemed to be at peace now. Everything was utter chaos then. Her thoughts meandered and she found herself drifting away....

∽

Most Mondays, while driving to work, Sanjukta took a familiar turn, a curve that connected one of the dark alleys to the main road. This was her favourite stretch.

School buses would crawl past and she would wave at the bobbing heads, trying desperately to peep from the window. Those smiles made Sanjukta's morning drive colourful and vibrant.

The lane across the pavement to her right opened to four little 'neighbourhoods'. She would slow down her car at each one of them. Four lives on the parallel road had become her extended family. A ritual. A routine. A tradition.

That day too, her foot hit the car's brakes, and Sanjukta's gaze was fixed at these four pockets that were like mushrooms popping out amid concrete and stones. Each mushroom opened up an umbrella of moments, some routine, others surprising. Sanjukta soaked in these moments daily. It was a story being written bit by bit, every day.

The florist stationed at the corner, a few metres from the gas station, watered his vivacious-looking flowers. Not that it equalled a garden of exquisite plant life, but it was enough for a lover to pick a red rose that would, perhaps later, wither away between the folds of his beloved's favourite romance novel.

Sanjukta was neither a lover, nor anyone's beloved. But flowers, she did love. Her husband, Nishit, would often bring her carnations. That was long time ago. Nishit had vanished, only the fragrance of a bittersweet marriage lingered. Sanjukta had moved on but the flowers had somehow remained.

The florist switched between his blue chequered and white polka-dotted shirt every alternate day. The sole pair of distressed jeans looked increasingly distressed, resigned to its fate, ready to breathe its last. Now that it was almost winter, he had pulled out a half-sleeved pyramid-patterned cardigan from his closet to keep himself warm.

'Why do you have that frown drawn across your forehead, Ajit?' Sanjukta asked the florist, rolling down her car window that morning.

'Madam, my flowers are sick because of this pollution. They don't smile any more,' Ajit replied, morose, sparing a glance at the dying sunflower.

Before Sanjukta could dispense a few words of solace, the traffic light changed to green. It signalled her to move on.

She moved on. Like always.

ﾩ

Mornings were misty and evenings were foggy. Nothing was poetic about either. *Delhi is wrapped in a sheet of hazardous smoke*, TV reporters and radio jockeys announced. Even newspaper headlines screamed doomsday for Delhiites. People were choking to death. Masks and oxygen cans were up for sale. Oxygen cans!

Sanjukta usually left early morning for work and returned late evening. Whenever she took the familiar turn towards her favourite stretch, she would find herself cutting through a film of dust and smoke. She slowed down at precisely four points during this morning exercise. She almost had the distance memorized—no, the number of speed breakers.

At the third speed breaker, the stench of fish would reach her nostrils even before the humble space of Neel's fish market appeared. She could, as usual, spot the indigo blue lungi being flaunted by the petite fish-seller. Sanjukta thought Neel's round eyes had started to bear an uncanny resemblance with one of his robust rohu fish. She would often think about it and laugh alone.

'Neelda, nice catch today it seems. How goes the business?' Sanjukta would throw her customary question at Neel every Wednesday and Friday.

'All good, Sanjuktadi, you must try my hilsa. Delicious and at a great discount. Even your cat will like it very much,' the fish-eyed Neel would chirp.

∽

From between the parting of the tattered tent cloth, Sanjukta saw the anklet on Shibu's mother's left foot. The ends of her green chiffon sari moved like a gentle breeze. The bedsheet was the same as day before, but her sari had changed, the anklet though was a permanent fixture. The second last stopover for Sanjukta was Shibu's tent. She adored the ten-year-old. He was smart, witty, and playful. And his mother, a perennial sleeping beauty. Well, that's how Sanjukta had always seen her, at least in the last ten days or so. Before that, going by hearsay, she had gone to her village to be with her parents. Shibu was all by himself. What a brave boy, Sanjukta had thought.

Does she sleep all day, all evening, oblivious to the outside world zooming past? In her sleep, she must have traversed countless years. Or, was it that she was only up and about in the afternoons, indulging her fatherless boy, tidying up her home, filling buckets of water, and cooking food on her dilapidated stove? All this, Sanjukta imagined while at work. She had never seen Shibu's mother awake. On her drive back home too, the scene would remain the same.

Who else did she have to call her own, who else did Shibu have to call his own? They owned each other.

∽

The florist was missing that morning. The roses and the lilies awaited an address. Their fragrances were wearing thin, the smog overpowered like a looming shadow. Will the lovers and beloveds buy these flowers that had been tainted by the cruel weather? The drooping yellow lily had lost hope of sunshine, the sunflower had forgotten to look to in the sky, the morning was like a shroud of evening. The flowers were tense, how long could they go on like this—the cluster of red roses, crimson chrysanthemums, the dirtied white lilies, dahlias that detested dalliance with the forceful toxic winds seemed to be in a conference of sorts.

But where had the florist disappeared?

∽

The last stop—Rishabh, the bangle-seller. He was busy counting the remaining glass bangles from his last stock of the red ones. 'Red is the colour of both anger and love. Isn't that peculiar, madam?' Rishabh had asked Sanjukta once. She was taken aback.

Sanjukta's meetings with these neighbourhoods were suspended on weekends. No office. No parallel reality.

Monday again, Sanjukta was late for work. She did not have time to stop by at any of the neighbourhoods.

Sanjukta wanted to talk to Shibu that evening. Diwali sweets were pending. She wanted to surprise him and his mother. On her way back from office, she stopped her car right next to Shibu's tent. She stepped inside, stealthily. The bedsheet was new. The mosquito net was rolled up in one corner. Everything looked all right, except one minor detail—the mother was missing. Sanjukta looked around, puzzled.

As if on cue, Shibu entered.

'Oh, Shibu, where were you? Look, I got you your favourite kaju katlis. Where is your mother?'

'I cremated her this afternoon. Been long pending.'

Cremated. Pending. These words dropped like bombs. What did he ever mean?

Sanjukta opened her mouth but no words would come out.

Shibu's tilted smile had shivers run down Sanjukta's spine.

'You know, I would often go to the gurdwara for the langar. I would leave early and return in the evening. That day, I didn't want to come back home to my dead mother.' Shibu began the story of a mishap.

'It's been over a week since she died. After midnight, I started visiting the nearby cremation ground to steal burnt wood. The dead deserve dignity. At least a shroud. My father abandoned us after I was born. He never returned to his wife and I never left his wife. She had coughed blood that night. But that was not unusual given that every winter, her lung condition would worsen. Eventually she would recover. This time, she didn't,' Shibu paused.

'But, why didn't you tell anyone. Did Neel know, what about Rishabh and Ajit?'

'Everyone knew. I would change her saris every day, and wash her body twice. She had three chiffon saris, anyway. Green, yellow, and red. I didn't have enough wood to cremate her, di.' Shibu's stoicism baffled Sanjukta.

'How could you survive like this for days on end, Shibu? Why didn't you tell me?' Sanjukta's voice was breaking. Lightning seemed to have struck her.

'It was getting cold, di. It would get colder after midnight. A corpse doesn't move, neither does it change sides, nor snore. I'd fall asleep wrapping myself around her. She was my quilt. *She kept me warm in this unforgiving cold.*'

When she heard this, Sanjukta turned pale. A dead body

as a shroud? The twinkling stars in the sky dimmed and she suddenly felt dizzy and giddy with fear, helplessness, and shock. Tears were stuck in her throat like a lump of dust and smoke.

Could this ever happen?

Shibu then led her to the corner behind the tent where he had been dumping stolen logs of burnt wood. She was choking while Shibu went about recounting his story.

'I collected enough wood with Rishabh and Neel's help. It was time to repay, give her the warmth she deserved. I know, I have been a selfish son. Now, tell me, do you think the pieces of wood that I gathered over the last week would have given her adequate warmth? But again, you didn't see the pyre, how would you guess?' Shibu asked, as he saw a frozen Sanjukta, her faraway glance now melting into and consumed by tears.

How could he be so matter-of-fact, dry, and yet so resolute?

That evening, she drove mindlessly. The speed breakers on her way made her car jump like a child on a trampoline. Each time her car leapt, her heart galloped. Yes, she did have the road memorized, but that evening, everything went helter-skelter, the foot on the car's accelerator did not budge. With every jerk, her tears came gushing out, the blood in her veins curdled, the fireflies in the sky danced the dance of death.

Sanjukta reached home frazzled. Slumping on the bed, she thought about the anklet on Shibu's mother's foot.

Wrapped in silken blankets, pillows, and satin sheets, Sanjukta was restless that night. She was feeling unbearably cold. She felt as if she lay on a bed of dry thorns. Even in absolute darkness, her trembling fingers searched for the switch to turn off the lights.

The cremation was over.

Should she go and ask Shibu how he was keeping himself warm, tonight?

It's not always about living in the margins, it's about living on the edge, too.

Tomorrow, she will ask the bangle-seller with a mole on his chin, 'Is there a colour of helplessness too?'

∽

Was it a dream or a nightmare? Everything was a blur.

Her head was throbbing. Nishit had hit her that night, so hard that she lost a tooth. And then, he had disappeared. Did he really think Shibu was dearer to her? Shibu had lost a mother and Sanjukta a spouse. Both were victims of doubt and helplessness.

Getting up, she stroked her cat, got ready and thought of stopping over at Neel's fish market. She and her cat had gotten used to the stench, after all.

SPIRITED NIGHTS

VIKRAM BALAGOPAL

There were nights Divya would switch off from the world and plant herself in the desolate courtyard behind her building to vape. There she would venerate the stars framed by the fronds of the coconut trees, imagining puffs of vapour rising up to them from her mouth and nostrils, as if her essence was escaping into the great void beyond.

Life is too dreary, she chimed in her head. There is no mystery to it. We are all suckers and conmen in the end. That is our pact with society, for it to function. So it was, that at her young age, she had lost her faith in humankind. She found some peace in solitude. On one of those warm, smoky nights, she dreamt a figure had roamed into her view of the stars. Female in its nakedness, gleaming in the moonlight, the figure stood on her wall. Their eyes locked, and she realized this was no dream.

Divya was a sculptor. Her life had begun as a prodigy at the age of nine. She recalled very little that came before. All that she knew and understood were the oohs and aahs the adults would make at her sketches. She recognized that her drawings were very different from those of the other children though she did not fully understand why. Her life became a series of performances making drawings for spectators. Her father held the reins at this point, having seen a good thing in his daughter's ability. 'Prodigy', they called her, on the TV programmes where she drew for the cameras. Speaking with strangers under harsh lights. And at home her mother and siblings would sit around and play the same programme on the TV. All she had wanted to do was to draw.

People insisted it was her passion. I am passionate about art, she parroted to herself and others. There was a well-rehearsed speech on her passion she made in interviews for various art schools around the world. The prodigy was welcome. The prodigy would get a scholarship. It felt natural that success would follow her shows. That her paintings would sell. But she soon grew bored of two dimensions. There was no more challenge there in getting the oohs and aahs. She started painting pottery. She then created the pots herself. Prodigy, they hailed. Ooh. Aah. She began to sculpt with her fingers. Ooh. Aah. All she had to do was follow her instincts and they would find the way along her arm down to a hand, the fingers, the wrinkled skin at the knuckles, the veins, the sinews of muscle flexing. Ooh, aah. Clay became too easy. Too soft. She procured a block of marble and chiselled away the surface to get to the form beneath. There was no undoing a mistake in marble. A misplaced chisel strike was forever. A blemish to a statue's nose was a blemished nose. A finger breaking off meant a four-fingered hand. Figure after figure was cast aside as she pushed a little too hard or struck the chisel at a mistaken angle. Finally, she had found the limit of her abilities. Discovering that she had a limit drove her close to madness.

She had never known failure. So in that defeat she reverted to painting. Her shows sold but no longer with the oohs and aahs. No longer was she hailed as extraordinary, visionary. Even sketching felt as difficult as algebra. These were the same fingers and she had the same head and mind. But she had lost her greatness somewhere along the way. Was it the curse of success?

She dared not return to marble. In a quest for another medium that might rekindle her lost passion she chanced upon metal. It was harder than stone and yet her 5-foot 2-inch body could tame it. Make it bend to her will. In her travels for research, she chanced upon a secret metal, thought lost to the ages. It became her secret to keep. She hid herself away in this lakeside godown she had converted into a forge and a workshop. To work at her metal. Once again earn those oohs and aahs that in her past life as a prodigy had come with so little effort. Now it took all the effort in the world. Without her passion to create, who was she? She asked herself that question most nights reclined in the canvas chair, gazing up at the stars.

And enter the naked woman on her wall. Their eyes were locked a long time. To Divya it felt like she was being taken stock of by a panther she had disturbed in its prowl. Was she in any danger, she wondered? Was this woman a burglar, or sneaking out to meet her lover? Or was this some deranged loon? And yet she found her hand rising. Her wrist flicked in a gesture to the stranger to join her on the ground. The woman bent down, the artist in Divya catching the flex of muscles on her thighs and shoulders as she crept off the wall, lowering herself until she clung on by a single hand. She raised her feet and was almost squatting on the surface of the wall like a tree frog. Then launched herself backward.

The naked woman lunged through the air, and all Divya did was blink. The next instant the woman vanished, mid-air. Divya had a vacant stare. Her heart was racing two hundred beats a minute. This was no ordinary woman she had encountered tonight. So the folk tales were true. She had been visited by the goddess of the lake.

Every night the next week, Divya waited in the courtyard, until finally on the ninth day she glanced up from refilling her vaping liquid and found the same female figure perched atop the wall. Divya sat up startled in her canvas chair. She hurriedly looked up again. Did she miss her? No, the woman was still there. Divya sat back and let out a sigh. Then they studied one another a while.

'My name is Divya,' she finally said, sucking at her vaporizer.

With a bemused tilt to her head, the woman on the wall replied, 'I know. You're a sculptor.'

It caught Divya off guard. She fought to steady her nerves.

'What is that metal you work with?'

Divya's mind was suddenly a blank. She searched desperately for the name, while the spirit carried on, 'I've never seen anything like it. The dark surface filled with marvellous light swirling stripes. It's almost like it's alive, or a slice of flowing water.'

'Wootz,' Divya barked at last.

'That's a strange name. I've never heard it before.'

Divya exhaled a long stuttering puff. 'It has a long history.'

'Oh?'

'And with a long history comes many names. The Europeans banned its production in the mid-1800s, and with that the traditional method was lost forever. Even the name Wootz is the mistranscription of an Anglicized version of the original Kannada word for steel—ukku. However true wootz is dead.'

She tried to stop there but found herself rambling on, 'Some of us have been trying to revive it. I source my ingots from a hobbyist in Salem, same as had been shipped from the Indian peninsula to Syria for at least a thousand years. Ukku, Hinduwani, seric iron, or as it was known by the famous blades it was shaped into in Syria—Damascus steel.'

'They used to make blades out of it? That must have been something to behold.'

The nights that followed were whiled away, seated in their respective spots, Divya in her canvas chair and the woman on the wall, discussing anything from theories about the universe, to music, books, and movies. But some nights, the spirit would arrive and she would lie there wordlessly, gazing starward, one leg dangling off the side. Divya would pretend to be as involved in the sky but through the drifting curls of vapour she could not help but observe this strange being visiting her night after night. Was there a reason?

Then one night, exhausted from pounding the hammer at work, Divya forced herself to stay alert by sipping a cup of strong black Arabica. So by the time the spirit finally arrived, Divya's head was swimming. Her eyelids fluttered to catch a glimpse of the spectral vision sauntering along the wall. She sat down, swinging her feet, humming. She noticed Divya getting up from her canvas chair and going into the flower bed beside the courtyard. Ten seconds later, Divya returned with a short stepladder, half-dragging it to the wall. The spirit stopped humming, watching Divya unfold it. It proved too short for her to climb up onto the wall. And yet, with each rung Divya climbed, entranced by the feet dangling within her reach, she smiled musing that, of course, a spirit would not shave her legs. Haltingly, her arms rose skyward. Her chest pressed up against the coarse brick wall covered in patches of green algae and an occasional slug.

The spirit did not move, merely peeping down past her knees at the approaching fingers trembling in anticipation. They hesitated an inch from her ankle. Paused. Then stroked her skin. Divya's head cocked, marvelling at making contact with a goddess, caressing the feet, a thumb grazing the grit from the bottom of those divine soles raining it down on to her own sweaty cheeks. She stroked the ankles, reaching up to the calves. The tips of her fingers could only go so far. Balancing on tiptoes atop the ladder, she nuzzled the feet, rubbing her cheeks over a top arch, rubbing her face, her nose, her lips against it, kissing at the skin that felt so real. You are real, she was thinking. I can feel you. You exist only on my wall, for me. You're real, only to me! Tears sprang from her clenched eyelids, smearing against the spirit's foot. Save me, she prayed.

Her right hand slowly lowered to her side. She reached behind her and brought out an object she had tucked into the waist of her pants. With glassy eyes admiring her goddess' face in the moonlight, she made an offering of a knife she had fashioned from wootz.

It was a ceremony she would repeat on the 19th of every month, presenting the goddess with a new blade. The smile she received was the only benediction she sought. And so it carried on. The tenth time, when after the spirit had leaned down from the wall and accepted the latest offering, she observed Divya holding an arm out to her. There was no hesitation on the part of the spirit. She reached down and pulled Divya up. For a while Divya sat quietly beside her, surveying the view. Then she turned, straddling the wall between her legs. The spirit echoed her movements. Facing one another there, Divya wondered at the accident of fate that had connected them. She yearned to touch and be touched. To explore and be explored. She held out her hand. Her fingers skated between the goddess's breasts, down her stomach. They flicked around the divine navel. Swimming deep in one another's eyes they leant forward meeting in a kiss, tasting, sucking at lips and tongues, licking inside the other's mouth. Divya's chest heaved. Her mouth rolled down the spirit's jawline to her neck. Her hands began to shake with a hunger, grabbing, stroking. Furiously the first time, calmer the second, painfully the third, they made love that night on the narrow brick wall that had bridged their existence.

The next night, Divya waited in tremulous anticipation, but the spirit did not arrive. Nights wore on to weeks. She stared alone at the sacred wall, reluctantly coming to terms with the possibility that the spirit might never visit her again. She knew in her heart that wherever she might be, she would never stop waiting, hoping to meet the spirit again. As she dove head first into creating new work, she felt her passion return. All those nights spent imploring the stars, the goddess had been their reply.

THE SMELL OF JOIPUR
LEISANGTHEM GITARANI DEVI

The dark night has slowly begun yielding to the first rays of the sun. Roosters from near and far promptly began crowing away full-throated. No one was more delighted than Saphabi upon hearing the roosters' call. The chimes of temple bells from afar too reassure her. She imagined the neighbourhood bamon walking hurriedly in small steps, clad in a small loincloth, and a white thread hanging loosely across his torso as he readies for the morning temple-ritual. Saphabi needs no other signs to announce the dawn of another morning. Never mind her mother's voice ringing to get her out of the bed!

'Saphabi, it is still dark outside! Don't even think of going out now.'

She overhears her father asking, 'Where is she going at this time?'

The woven bamboo wall separating their rooms easily gives away the hushed talks.

As if her father is unaware of where she is going! As if he does not know what young girls of her age do during Yaoshang!

She has been long ready, dressed in her new red phanek and her joipur. All she needs now is one blind moment of courage to dash outside. That's it!

As soon as she woke up, she somehow managed to

The Smell of Joipur

grope her way in the dying light of the lantern kept in the deity Sanamahi's corner—crossing her parent's bed, then her grandmother's bed, then the kitchen, and finally reached the backyard where water was stored. Searching for the lone, overworked mug was another challenge in the dark. She had reminded her mother many times to buy one more mug. But where is she listening!

Every morning, she manages to pull herself out of the bed only after her mother's wake-up alarm blares through the half earthen, half bamboo walls and rings out into the passage that runs right from the front door to the back door: '*SAPHABI*...are you still sleeping? Are you asking me to come?'

Such questions are not to be mistaken for affection. Her mother has to simply issue her threat from whichever part of the house she may be in, and out they spring from the bed.

Today was different. There was no need for her mother's siren to make her leap out of the bed. She has been eagerly waiting for this day. This is the only time of the year when young girls can wear a joipur and a matching phanek.

The smell of joipur lingers in her memory. Rows of colourful joipur stacked up in the local women's market beckon the coming of Yaoshang. The smell of fresh colourful flower prints on starched white cloth remains a fond memory even when one grows older. In this festival of colours, young girls visit the houses in the locality asking for money from people as nakatheng. They can even stop pedestrians or motorists and demand money from them. All is fair in Yaoshang!

Yaoshang is a festival for all. Old men get drunk. Old women immerse themselves in Chaitanya Mahaprabhu's devotion. Young women—married or unmarried—feast during the day. At night, they come out in their finest clothing and rejoice at the Thabal-chongba—dancing round and round to the drumbeats and the tune of wind instruments, holding young men's hands. Like it or not, this is the only time in the year when boys proudly roam the streets armed with all sorts of colours and water guns. While the boys busy themselves in scaring young girls with their water guns and colours, young girls busy themselves in collecting nakatheng from houses nearby and afar.

Once Yaoshang is over, one loses the right to ask for nakatheng. Even the lovely joipur loses its charm once the festival is over. Even if one were to wear it, things were never the same. Saphabi's endearing joipur too ends up greasy in the corner of the table where the cooking stove is mounted. Sometimes it finds its way to her father's shoeshine collectibles.

Years of experience have taught Saphabi and her friends to avoid known misers and dog-keepers. Some houses are known for giving only ten paisa in this day and age! Saphabi shrugged and said one time, 'I would rather brave the dogs than make a mockery of myself with the ten paisa these rich people had to offer.'

Unfortunately, on the same day when they went for nakatheng, an unfriendly black dog snarled at them. Everyone in the group fled in all directions, like bees flying from a honeycomb struck with a stone. Saphabi's courage too vanished in the face of the ferocious dog. This was during the previous Yaoshang. This year the girls hope for better.

She has already wasted a larger part of the morning dreaming up the events of the day. Saphabi and her friends had planned everything in detail the previous evening—that they will first cover the neighbourhood houses, and the following morning they would visit the relatives. They can

The Smell of Joipur

accumulate more money only after relatives have loosened their purse strings. This is why the girls promised each other that they should make an early start the next day to cover great distances.

Yet here she is, still at home wondering how to muster the courage to get out.

'Saphabi, Saphabi, why haven't you still come out?'

Lata stood on her toes and craned her neck across the bamboo gate. Lingjel's and Bina's excited voices could be heard too.

Saphabi can hear nothing else now. She darts out of her house, leaving behind a still yelling mother.

Lata admonishes her, 'You said you will come out very early! Is this *your* early?'

'Assh,' Saphabi sighs in protest. Lata can never understand her.

Saphabi has a sister who is entirely the opposite of her. She is what-people-call 'homely' type—pretty, endearing, and protected. She does not roam around everywhere for nakatheng. The truth is her sister does not think it fit to join her younger sister's group, and her own friends are a bit too old for such endeavours. This is why she is driven indoor most of the time while her younger sister is let loose 'like a stray calf', in her mother's words.

Saphabi once protested, 'Ima, why do I always have to accompany your older daughter? Can she not go on her own? You might as well worship her in a glass box.'

One of her distant uncles had once joked, 'Iche, you can easily find a groom for your older daughter even with one eye closed. Sigh, but you have to gift a truck to whoever your younger daughter marries!'

One day, when her grandmother was waiting for the

school van holding one granddaughter's hand in one hand and the other in another, a woman from the locality came up to them and remarked, 'Oh my! Who is this ugly child? Not at all like her elder sister!' Saphabi howled and refused to step into the school van. Poor old woman, after much embarrassment, she has learnt to praise Saphabi's 'good' looks every time she sees her.

As her older sister chooses to stay at home all the time with a stoic disinterest in community affairs, Saphabi endures the status of being an uncontrollable girl. She couldn't help feeling a bit edgy at Lata's taunting.

'I am the only one awake so early to get out of home. Everyone is still in bed. My sister is also still in bed. So Ima stopped me from coming out so early,' said Saphabi.

Saphabi's feisty wings are always clipped to the size of her sister's. Sometimes it is confusing for her. When her mother needs her to run errands for her, Saphabi transforms to a fearless one. When, however, she wants to go out with her friends, she is scolded for being a wayward girl. In fact, she is often told to 'behave like your sister'.

Despite everything, she manages to slither out from her mother's hold. The scolding was yesterday, and today is a new day, she thinks. So this morning again she is out with her friends.

Lata, Bina, Lingjel, and Saphabi jauntily marched forward, climbing up the riverbank on this misty, exciting morning. Saphabi is confident her aunt will make her very proud. She is the most generous relative, after all.

One thing troubles her though. However early it is, they might encounter boys laden with aber. It dirties her face and her clothes. On such occasions, she is thankful for her unattractive features. For, the boys mostly target the prettier ones. Lata hilariously ends up having the most darkened face.

The uneven muddy path to her aunt's house seemed longer than usual. The danger of being hit by water balloons and being surrounded by boys increases in longer distances. Saphabi could see some women climbing up the steep riverbank balancing their brass pitcher on their hips. 'They can probably save us from the boys,' she thought. As the women scaled the steep riverbank, Saphabi wondered how they even walk up to their house, all wet and water dripping from their phanek. It is still cold, after all.

When they reached her aunt's house, her aunt was hurrying to finish her morning ritual in a wet phanek wrapped around her chest. A piece of white muslin cloth was placed on her head as a mark of respect to both the gods and men in the family.

She was doing her morning tulsi puja. As though she has been expecting her niece, she says: 'Heima! Are you here already? Here, sit for some time. Have you been to other places?'

'No, yours is the first one. Nene, please give us lots of money. This time we are going to eat ilisha.'

'Thida! What a crazy girl!' says her aunt affectionately.

'Bring my nakatheng fast; we have to cover other places too! Last time we fell short of money and Ima had to put more money into our collection. I know this time she will refuse to give any more.'

'OK, wait here.'

Saphabi nervously waits for her aunt to come out with the money. As expected, she sees a fifty-rupee note in her aunt's hand. The girls happily took the money and stood up to go.

'I am going to the other houses next door. You think they will give me lots of money?' Saphabi asks her aunt. Her aunt's relatives did try to match up to her expectations. Each of them gave her ten rupees. The girls happily left the place and started walking toward the riverbank, heading now for Bamon Leikai where Bina's grandparents live.

The way to Bina's grandparents' house is full of challenges. Not only is it very far, the entire stretch of the road is filled with street heroes. It is most hateful for the girls. As it is, the sun is already shining bright and hunger pangs have started kicking in. The delectable food that they will eat at the end of this run is what keeps them going.

Lingjel suggests, 'Let's have tea and pafor from one of the shacks, I am very hungry. I can barely pull myself any further.'

The more worldly-wise Lata objects, 'If we spend before we collect a sufficient amount, how will we raise money for the feast?'

Saphabi is in two minds. She certainly does not mind a little something to eat. Her stomach has been growling for quite some time now. However, Lata being the older one usually has a greater say on matters pertaining to the welfare of the group.

By the time they reached Bina's grandparents' house, they are ready to faint with hunger. Bina's grandmother was busy picking out weeds from her kitchen garden. Saphabi nudges her friend to ask her grandmother for something to eat. But the shrewd girl pretends not to have heard her friend. As it is people in Manipur do not indulge in snack culture. They eat their big meal only two times—one in the morning and the other in the evening—and the rest of the day is forgotten in their work. Therefore, Bina's grandmother also didn't offer them anything to assuage their hunger.

On the way back, even the usually controlled Lata succumbed to the churning hunger. The long walk up and down, and the manoeuvres to elude the colour-sporting boys, have already worn them down. How will they even manage to reach other places!

Thinking of the long morning ahead, Lata is now willing to spare some money and feed themselves.

'Abok, give us tea and pafor,' says Lata.

The shack where they chose to have tea is no different from the other tea shacks that stand along the road. It is a run-down, lopsided structure. The walls are but just a reminder of its older duty-worn self. What remains of the earthen wall is the skeletal frame made of bamboo. Even worse is the tea seller—an old woman bent more by her duties than by her age. Lata couldn't have chosen a better tea stall than this! Surprisingly, the place seems to be more crowded than any other is. Maybe the well-stocked plates of bora and 'Lizzat' papad are attracting the crowd. 'What is Yaoshang without bora and pafor after all,' exclaimed Saphabi. Other eatables are also popular around this time, but the girls prefer eating papad because it is cheap.

After an endless wait, the old woman brings a plate of papad and the glasses of tea. What a delight it is! The papads vanished as a handful of salt would in the Loktak.

'Abok, your pafor is very tasty. Give us some more.'

'How much will you eat!' scolds Lata.

True, Saphabi is fond of eating. Even her dainty sister keeps taunting her for nibbling away whatever snacks their mother brings home 'like a rat'. But this does not disconcert Saphabi. She often quarrels with her sister on food. However, she cannot fight Lata. Grudgingly she gets up to resume the mission with an unsatisfied tummy.

As they near the Singjamei Bridge, the girls can see some boys leaning against the railing of the bridge. They appeared harmless—no colour and no water balloons. The girls did not bother to hide or wait for the boys to leave. As they draw nearer, one of the boys says:

'The girl in blue phanek, may I ask your name? I would very much like to be your friend.'

Lingjel glowed in her blue phanek. Typically, a smile escapes her face.

Another boy says, 'But my heart is set on the beauty in yellow phanek.'

Lata looks far from being pleased and pretends she did not hear anything at all.

Saphabi cannot help feeling humiliated and rejected, even though she is not alone in this. As though this rejection were not enough, one of the boys jocularly comments:

'Our friend in red phanek looks like she is from a family that owns a huge granary. She herself resembles a sack of grain.'

THAT'S IT.

Saphabi charges toward the boy like a mad bull and grabs him by his shirt. She then flings the shocked boy to the ground. Saphabi pins him down to the ground by placing her right foot onto his chest. No one could have anticipated such a violent turn. Everyone freezes! In the next second, Saphabi's friends pulls her back from the helpless boy writhing under her foot. Her hands are still wildly reaching out for him in the air and feet still kicking the unfortunate fellow. The boy's friends helped him up—shocked, shaken, and humiliated. He must have been wondering if this were a dream!

Her grandmother had always told her, 'Nothing is more beautiful than knowledge.'

But Saphabi's young mind is troubled. With neighbours, relatives, and even friends having fun at the expense of her looks, her tender heart is hurt. Many times, she had tried wearing the dresses that looked so enviably pretty on her sister. But the same dresses looked ill-fitting on her—the back side of the dress always longer than the front that struggles so hard to cover her protruding belly.

Now, this boy has touched the very nerve that shakes her entire soul and that too in front of her friends! She is relentless and she feels the boy has rightly deserved every inch of the pain she has caused him.

Lata scolds her, 'Eeesh! What an embarrassment you are! Why do you have to fight like that? I am never going out with you.'

Saphabi is unrelenting.

'Fine! I will also not join the feast. Did you not see how that boy was making fun of me? Won't you also beat him up if he teases you?'

Of course, Lata will do no such thing! Adding salt to the injury is her name—SAPHABI—the healthy one.

Lata once said, 'Saphabi, when your face becomes red, you look like a coal drum wrapped in a cloth.'

Saphabi became so angry that she came back home leaving their game midway. Another time, she told Saphabi she looks like an over-fried bora.

This is not the first time Saphabi has beaten up somebody. She has quite a history of beating up people who make fun of her or anybody from her family. Once she pulled out the hair of a girl who taunted her sister. Instead of being thankful to her younger sister, she threw such a fit!

'I am never going out with your younger daughter. She is embarrassing! She starts fighting with anyone that says anything to her!'

Even Lata has refused to be her friend now. Disappointing as this may be, Saphabi has to save her face. She fought with Lata, demanded her share of the luncheon fund, and stormed back home all alone.

Her mother was washing clothes in the courtyard when she reached home, the sun shining bright on the aluminium washtub.

'Eh! Isn't it too early for you to be home?' taunts her mother.

Saphabi went inside without a word. She dashed straight for her bed, still sulking.

She got even more agitated when her mother called her to come and eat food. Hasn't she noticed yet she is upset? The entire protest is weakened at the mention of food. Even as she is battling whether to nurse her ego or shame herself by giving into food, she could hear the blaring sound of the loudspeaker announcing the beginning of the Yaoshang sports. A sense of loss suddenly sinks in. She is missing all the fun in the Yaoshang sports ground. Yet she has convinced herself she is never going out with Lata and the group any more. She enters the kitchen and tells her mother: 'Ima, if Lata and all come to call me, tell them I am busy reading. I don't want to play with them any more.'

Her mother wonders! Yet she says, 'All right, come and eat your food at least.'

'I am not hungry now. I will eat later.' Saying this, she goes back to bed again.

In the afternoon when Saphabi's mother was picking up the clothes from the bamboo clothes-line, she could hear

Lata asking her mother, 'Nene, where is Saphabi?'

'Oh, she....' Before her mother could even complete the sentence, Saphabi rushes out of the house.

'Are you going to the Yaoshang sports ground? I am also coming,' announces Saphabi excitedly without waiting for an answer.

Saphabi's mother says affectionately, 'Don't come back home fighting again, OK?'

Saphabi didn't reply. She was busy enquiring who all were participating in what sport activity.

Her mother watches her daughter says affectionately, wondering what will become of this feisty girl! As she inserts the bamboo poles into the slotted wooden pillars that serve as the gate, she continues watching out for her daughter, full of life and promise, heading towards the riverbank.

REFLECTIONS ON A COMMON JOURNEY
NEERA KASHYAP

Dandelion. It comes several times in my dreams. In hard earth stretching dull and brown into the horizon. An olive-green stem wavers uncertainly in the wind, then straightens, its crown flat and round. It is a bud. Its enclosing leaves thrust upwards, delicate and weak, holding the secret of the flower within. The leaves try to open but close tight around the secret. Open, close. In one dream, I find I am awake—watching. The leaves twitch open a little, jerk, and close tightly around the bud.

At first, I thought the dandelion was cannabis. But a Google search showed cannabis to have a cluster of long leaves—strong and green, serrated to the tip. Its flower sprung up from within the cluster like a sprig of orchid. White, mottled blue. Anuj's eyes were mottled red. I assumed it was lack of sleep. His tongue moved over dry lips in a strange snaky glide. I assumed it was a fear of exams, his last two semester grades had dropped drastically. His appetite had increased but he ate more clumsily, dropping cutlery, spilling food. I assumed Manoj made him even more nervous with his army ways, his overkill with stories of war heroics. Anuj seemed to look at me as if out of a cloud, his eyes straining to focus, to speak. Where are your books, Anuj? Where is your squash racket? Where are your friends? His eyes squinted as if they would take longer to comprehend what I was saying. His smelt of smoke.

Finally, I track it to his bedroom. A smoky smell of rotting oranges, stronger in the toilet. Inside the cabinet, propped against the side wall was Manoj's cigar box, packed with green leaves like chopped herbs. I smell them with rising dread. A drug? An intoxicant? No. No. This couldn't be a drug...there was no drug history in my family. Neither in Manoj's. Both families belonged to the Services—generations of men had served in the Army, the Air Force. With pride, with honour, with spilled blood. Where did this green thing come from? This...this wildness?

Those were innocent days. Manoj used strong arm tactics, bellowed, 'Stop this, you hear? No son of mine will be a druggie.' He slapped Anuj hard, his finger marks appearing like a rash across the boy's pale face, prickling red. Manoj's face prickled redder, mottled with hurt and anger. He belted Anuj again and again, repeating: 'No son of mine will be a druggie,' till he exhausted himself. This strategy took months to burn itself out. By the time we took Anuj to a drug treatment centre, he had moved to heroin. That night I dreamt of him walking to the edge of a cliff—a tall gaunt figure, curly haired, shuffling, desolate. He is wearing a pair of black shorts striped with green. I watch him, wave to his back, scream something but no sound comes. I cannot move. A swarm of dandelion stems have twisted around my feet, holding them down.

5

Harm reduction drugs. This buprenorphine—harmless, white, and round. Bitter as hell. It makes me shit and spew at the same time. My legs feel like thick iron rods. I barely make it to the wash basin—spew at its edge, watch the brown gruel splatter from my mouth to the floor. Small wet gobs fall on my T-shirt. I should change but don't have the energy. I stretch out on the cool floor, feel my head spin slowly with the speed of the fan. The wet gobs dry on my chest, mix with the stench of sweat. This buprenorphine is supposed to reduce the craving but all I can feel is an urge to use, use, use. Even a smoke of plain weed would be good. Blissful, like the colours of a peacock's fan, shimmering in the breeze, loving...joyful...making me feel safe as a house...as a mountain.

My heart races with need, my iron legs shudder. Eyes close. Getting fucked up on drugs wasn't the plan. It was smoking at parties—harmless stuff, the guys said. Then we rolled more into the paper so we could compare the highs. Blood raced like a raging river. When the river slowed, there was panic—no cause, just panic. The smell of fear in sweat. Sweat disobeying the seasons—cold sweat when blistering hot, hot when bloody cold. Nothing obeys me. How do I explain this to Dad when he stands in his uniform and takes off his belt? That nothing obeys me. It was good for many months. Then a switch in the brain flipped from normal to addict, and nothing obeys. Nothing. Mom looks at me with those huge eyes of her, appealing, compelling, blazing. She steals into my room some nights and whispers one of her mantras into my ear. She thinks it will work on my subconscious. She doesn't know I am fully awake—I can barely sleep more than a few hours at a time. Your mumbles won't work, Mom. Nothing obeys. Nothing.

∽

Manoj took up a posting to a non-family station, leaving me alone to face this war. He was used to being obeyed, couldn't stomach disobedience. Said as soldiers, there were just three options at war: to kill, to get killed, and to return safely. He didn't think much of prisoners—the caged ones whose futures looked bleak and unheroic.

The buprenorphine worked well for a while as a substitute for heroin. But it wasn't enough. It kept Anuj at this mellow stage until he could get to the next drug, fix, whatever they call it.

I liked the doctor at the second treatment centre. He changed the drug, saying something about buprenorphine being a partial agonist unlike methadone which was a full agonist. Anuj now needed a full agonist so some receptors in his brain could be stimulated more against the craving. As he spoke, I half watched Anuj perform asanas under a yoga instructor in a hall beyond the doctor's alcove. As his body contorted so did his face. When flat on his back in shavasana, his body twitched.

The doctor's voice rose: 'Many people believe that addiction is purely psychological and can be stopped at will. Because it begins with a voluntary act, they think it cannot be called a disease. It is true, addiction starts voluntarily but what follows is such a complex neurochemical cascade that it makes addiction a disease rather than a conscious choice. Changes take place in the brain over time. The person loses control when earlier he could exercise control. The behaviour becomes compulsive and uncontrollable like other brain diseases. Parkinson's patients cannot control their trembling, nor can schizophrenics control their hallucinations. So a user needs both medical treatment and psychosocial intervention. Psychosocial intervention alone will not work.'

The others in the yoga group had risen. Anuj still lay in shavasana. The instructor hovered over him for a second, then moved away to demonstrate the next asana to the others. I turned to look at my hands lying limp in my lap. I was startled to see how deeply I had chewed on my nails. More exposed skin than nail. I reached for my bag with trembling hands. There were changes taking place in more than one brain. The agony...the agonist from partial to full.

I dreamt that night of a rat. I tried to kill it with a broom shaped like a giant dandelion. The more I hit it, the more it turned into a baby. The baby wouldn't die. I cried because I was trying to kill it. At the end, I just kept the rat/baby. I woke up, sweaty with dread.

∽

Methadone. Thick green liquid. Bitter as hell. But it's working. It's as if there is a ceiling on the high, but it's still a high. There is less pain in the body, less craving for the fix. The dark circles under the eyes have gone. At least I don't look like an addict. That doc is a pain, sure, keeps talking about reducing the dose but this methadone stuff is working. I am not getting and using, getting and using. Don't have to hunt out those rat agents. In shady holes. This comes home, all clean, prescribed. I feel dopey but it's nothing compared to the drug haze of active scoring. If I can stay clean and do what is asked, there is no big deal. I am back at college for classes, pretending everything is normal. Mohit winks from the front row—he knows, the dope.

∽

The doctor said methadone was addictive and that the drug had to be reduced. Anuj couldn't take the reduction. He said his bones felt like lead. It wasn't what Anuj said but what happened to him when taken off the drug and put on something else that made my hair stand on end. He sweated, he vomited, he hallucinated, he walked about through the night like a ghost, he suffered from chills and fever and stomach cramps. He veered towards depression. He was put back on methadone. He overdosed. Deliberately and knowingly. He stole money from my purse so he could buy more through a legal prescription. I didn't empty my purse of money for I knew he would find other ways to get the... the drug. He had to be admitted to a residential rehab so his dosage could be monitored. We went through the paces of psychosocial counselling. But no one was listening. The doctors were more interested in addiction test results by what they jovially call 'parking the patient in medicines'. Anuj was more interested in getting enough methadone to stay afloat. I was more interested in my prayer beads, in my dandelion dreams for signs of hope, in figuring out calm in the throes of a mind that screeched back information: increasing methadone can be ineffective in the long run—can create drastic mood swings, can increase the need for more opioids, can cause withdrawal symptoms, can be stored in the body so you become dependent on it like another organ.

I decided to have a haircut followed by a meal at a Chinese restaurant. Alone. There was no one I could eat with. I was alone, as alone as Anuj was alone.

ல

This rehab is a prison. All that spiel of cognitive-behavioural psychotherapy and psychodynamic treatments. I wait for my doses of methadone brought to me by a bearded nurse who slaps down the capfuls as if she was throwing off poison. If I ask for more, she flies off the handle and brings in the head matron who gives me a mouthful on the sins of the flesh. The counsellor is no better. He spends barely five minutes—only to lecture me on my urges and how I must beat them for the sake of my family and society. I don't matter because I am a pariah. A low life. I was ill and I can say I'm still ill and I will be ill up to the end of my life. Methadone is just an alternative to heroin. With heroin, the pain would start at 1-2 p.m., with methadone it starts earlier. First, the feet become sore, then the back aches, and I feel itchy all over. Within five minutes of taking the stuff, I am fine. The high comes more slowly, but it comes—slowly but surely. It's in between doses that it gets bad. Really bad. Thoughts come screeching like monkeys. I feel empty in my soul when I look at myself, feel an aversion for what I see. If I could take the stuff when I want and how much I want, I wouldn't feel this emptiness, this sinking. Maybe I'll tell the doc I am scoring again so he will increase my dose of methadone. So I can sleep.

I miss Mom. Mom with her prayer beads, her eyes that don't blaze that much—just looking sad and sunk in. Maybe she also feels empty...or plain quiet. She is thinner, looks much older than when I started five years ago. She is around. She doesn't complain. If it wasn't for her and for methadone, I would have been dead.

∽

I sometimes wake up among the dandelions as I dream of them. Still closed, still withholding the secret of the flower within. I am awake. I watch calmly as I walk among a field of dandelions. There is one ahead of me—straight, not waving in the breeze. Its leaves move to open, then close. The stem thrusts up, now taller than the rest, opens slowly and a vibrant yellow flower unfolds. Its long delicate petals bob in the wind. I watch the leaves gather around in an orchestrated dance, enfold the yellow creature till it closes in a bud, not flat but curving upwards to the sky. I find I am without any thought. Just watching. Calm.

A month later I dream again of the bud. The same bud dandelion, taller than the rest of the closed sprigs. I am awake again and look at it this time with affection. It opens. It opens not as a yellow flower but as a seed head, white. It opens like a fan, top down, till it is round as a globe. It is a web of delicate shivering filaments carrying seeds. I know it will be blown away by the breeze any minute. In full wakefulness, I whisper to it: 'Seed love where you fly. Let love seed in this arid desert.' The little globe is pulled to one side by the breeze, separates from the stem and floats into space like a misshapen little cloud.

It's after breakfast that I get a WhatsApp message from Anuj. It is a link to something. I double click on the link. It opens to a beautiful building of Portuguese architecture set in a scenic landscape with lakes, rivers, rice fields, and thick natural vegetation. The e-brochure says it is a 'tertiary residential treatment for clients who have either attended primary treatment facilities on aspects of substance abuse, de-addiction, and relapse prevention, or managed recovery by other means. For those recovering from addiction, it is also a space for tertiary treatment in mental health after primary care or detox. Our work is distinct for we adopt a multi-disciplinary approach that encompasses psychotherapy with a lot of self-exploration through art, didactic lectures, first-hand experiences of nature, and travel therapy involving cultural immersion. We take our guests for heritage walks, gallery openings and encourage self-expression through creative writing. We encourage the presence and participation of family members so that healing takes place through supportive parental care and understanding.'

∽

We sit in a room with old elegant furniture, vibrant woven dhurries, and framed paintings of people and natural beauty. The slatted windows are wide open. The sound of the river enters the room, lulls its occupants. There are 'clients', some with a parent or parents, some without. People here have come from all parts of the world. But the group is small. We sit in a circle on ancient cushioned chairs with broad backs and arm rests, the lead consultant—a gentle bearded psychotherapist—sitting relaxed among us. I have listened wide-eyed to people read their stories, poems, reflections— not just clients but parents too. I am nervous when it comes to my turn, stutter I have nothing to say just yet. I am more nervous for Anuj who sits slouched, half asleep. He has no paper in front of him, no notebook. My heart hammers for him.

When his turn comes, he sits up, fully alert. His curled head bends forward as he looks down intently into his phone. Not the phone, not now, Anuj, I urge silently. He says he wants to read a poem that he liked a lot. It came this morning as a WhatsApp forward. He holds up his phone to show the group the logo under which the poem features—Wilder Child—a red-filled circle with two white palms joined at the thumbs, held outwards at a slant. It is by a poet named Nicolette Sowder and has no title, he says. He takes a deep breath and reads:

May we raise children
who love the unloved

Reflections on a Common Journey

> things—the dandelion, the
> worms and spiderlings.
> Children who sense
> the rose needs the thorn.

He pauses for a moment, his brow knotted. His brow clears. He reads on:

> and run into rainswept days
> the same way they
> turn towards the sun...

> And when they're grown and
> someone has to speak for those
> who have no voice
> may they draw upon that
> wilder bond, those days of
> tending tender things
> and be the ones.

THE PIMP

SUBHASH CHANDRA

Since the time he attained consciousness, he found himself in the company of the old beggar, whom he called Baba and a street dog, Kallu, who was the beggar's pet. The beggar had found the newly-born twins—a boy and a girl—near the Railway Goods Yard in front of GB Road (Garstin Bastion Road), a red-light area in Delhi. It was freezing cold and the babies had turned blue. The old man covered them with all the rags he had. But only the boy survived. The three of them lived on the measly food the beggar's alms could muster.

When the child was four years old, the beggar died. He began wandering around GB Road with Kallu in tow. All sorts of shops function on the ground floors, while the remaining three floors are kothas, each run by a bai. The shopkeepers knew him. They had seen the old man carry him as a baby in his arms.

In the daytime, the shops transact business as in any other market with no clue to the uninitiated what the rundown three floors above the shops house. After sunset these houses come alive in garish colours, sharp scents, and liquor smell. Entry is from the rear along a narrow potholed road, where the pedestrians have to zigzag their way through the cycle rickshaws, autos, and handcarts. The customers go up the perpetually damp and stinking staircases whose walls are stained red with betel spit. Primal male sex drive is what makes life bustle and throb in the kothas.

∽

The child grew up to be eleven years old.

In the day, many of the prostitutes stood in the balconies watching the flow of life on the road with which they were barely in touch. They were not allowed to go out into the city without an escort (the muscleman) of the bai. That was the only source of diversion, but it was occasional.

One day a woman called out to him. 'Chhotu, come up.' She sent him to buy a bottle of scented oil. When he came back, she gave him a twenty-five paisa coin.

He got a name that day.

Over time, the bai and the other prostitutes of this kotha—one of the largest with twelve women—began to get sundry things from the market through Chhotu and he became an errand boy. The bai allowed him a corner in the kotha, which was not visible to the customers, as the sight of a piteous child could dampen the intensity of their urge to have sex. He was scrawny, his face poky and pale, his eyes sunken and teeth discoloured. Kallu was not allowed upstairs. He loitered around on the road, but whenever he spotted Chhotu, he would vigorously wag his tail and follow him.

Chhotu thus became a part of the grimy world where the chipped and decaying buildings were in sync with the chewed up and sapped bodies of the whores. They talked, joked, laughed, and teased each other, and flirted crassly with the visitors to lure them. But they were scraped out from inside. Occasionally, one would shed silent tears in solitude for her family, lost forever.

The bai was well fed, sported gold ornaments, and spoke in a commanding voice. The women were in awe of her and obeyed her unquestioningly. Chhotu would be around in the day as a handy boy till the women got busy decking themselves up with cheap cosmetics for the business at night. Then he was dispatched to his hidden corner. But Chhotu did not go to sleep for a long time and avidly watched the goings-on.

It was natural, therefore, for him to attain puberty rather early. He liked a particular girl whose smile was charming and filled him with joy. But he knew he had to suppress the urge or else the consequences would be disastrous! He might lose his shelter and would have to beg like his Baba.

However, one day he could not control himself. The object of his desire was cooking. He went and sat by her side.

'Kya re, Chhotu, you have nothing to do?'

'No,' he said and looked at her in a way she was too familiar with. She decided to have a little fun with him.

'How do you like it here, Chhotu?' she asked.

'Good.'

She raised her eyebrows in mirth.

'I mean, it's nice in here,' he said smiling awkwardly.

'What's so nice in here?'

He looked around cautiously. But the word got stuck in his gullet.

'Chhotu, bol?'

Suddenly, the word flew out of his mouth like a stone from a catapult: 'You.'

She gave a tinkling laugh.

He felt encouraged and held her soft breast. His body trembled with the electric pleasure that coursed through him.

She smiled, gently removed his hand, and pinched his ear. 'First get big enough, idiot.'

The Pimp

How to convince her that he was big enough? How to tell her he could make love to her as no one else could? But she sent him on an errand, and that was the end of the session, and his hope.

∽

Then Chhotu turned seventeen.

His sex drive had bloomed. At times, he soaked in life at the kotha into the wee hours. In the day time, he saw women moving about half-clad, careless with their bodies in front of him, sending him into convulsions. But even now none of them took him seriously. Though he had his favourite, now he lusted after all the women.

One afternoon, one of them had gone to the terrace to pick up the clothes she had put on the line for drying. He stealthily enfolded her from behind.

The woman pushed him away, irritated. 'Have you gone mad, Chhotu?'

Not one of them would let him come close. He was confused. What was wrong with him? When he was small, some of them played games with him on the terrace and even fondled him. He had gone out of his way to help several of them by getting medicines in the midnight January chill, or buying tea leaves, betel nuts, and sundry items in the blazing June sun. But none obliged him.

The frequency of his desire increased and so did the trips to the roofless bathroom on the terrace where he managed relief by himself.

Two more years passed.

Chhotu was promoted. One day, as he was returning from the market, a first-timer made an enquiry and he brought him up to the kotha. That day, from an errand boy he became a pimp. The regular pimp had grown old and the bai had been mulling replacement as he could not muster enough customers. She gave Chhotu a chance and he proved his mettle. He had learnt the ropes quickly from life at the kotha and his gift of the gab helped him. The number of clients shot up. He continued to be called Chhotu and still slept at the kotha. Everyone was happy—the bai, the whores, and Chhotu himself.

∽

Years kept adding height and muscle to his body. The onset of youth and a regular income had filled out his face and emaciated body and he looked presentable. Chhotu became a man.

He had developed a knack of sizing up a potential customer. He would approach casually and begin to work on him in whispers. His sensual, erotic descriptions of the voluptuous fairies at the kotha made six or seven out of ten clients follow him. He became an expert pimp envied by his ilk.

But there were times when he hated himself. He was aware of all the sordidness that lay behind this tinsel, putrid world. He had gotten to know how these once innocent girls were tricked and brought here from far-flung, hunger-stricken villages in West Bengal, Jharkhand, and even Nepal. False promises about jobs with a rosy future in Delhi, and fake marriages—charades in which the parents were often complicit for a measly sum—threw the girls into this blazing hell. He had also been privy to the miserable stories of some of the women, who wistfully talked about their families, forever lost.

Over the years, he had seen nubile girls with welts and

The Pimp

bruises for refusing to get initiated. Brutal beating, solitary confinement, denial of food for days on end, and finally sometimes the muscleman—at the behest of the bai—forcing himself on her, broke a girl's resistance. He could not forget the expression on the face of a new girl going into a cubicle for the first time, looking like a goat on way to the slaughterhouse.

Enticing men—sometimes trapping an innocent passerby by titillating his libido—engendered guilt in him.

The bai liked him, no doubt, but still she often cheated him on the commission by reducing the number of customers he had brought on a particular day.

'You were lucky you survived. Your sister could not,' Baba had told him one day.

Lucky?

He missed his dead sister and tried to visualize her face. But the faces of the women at the kotha floated before his eyes. He shuddered! It was just as well she was dead. But for days, he continued to think of her and felt dejected.

Once he dreamed of her. She did not look like any of the women he brought up customers for. Thank God!

She came and sat silently on the cot and smiled. He was thrilled that he had a sister! But then a dread gripped him. How did she get his address? Did she know what kind of a place this was? Yes, she did. She held his hand and led him down the stairs. She wanted to take him out of here, to a decent, clean, respectable place. Suddenly, a truck trundled down the road. In a flash, she pushed him aside but lay mangled herself. She had died a second time to save him! He sat up awake and wept bitterly.

∽

'What's it, Chhotu? You're still lolling on the cot. It's time to get to work and bring customers,' said the bai.

'I'm not going today.'

'Why?' The bai was surprised.

'Don't feel up to it.'

She smiled amusedly. 'Very good! This evening the seth is not in a mood to work.'

He did not respond.

'Come on and get going. Or else we would be losing out on clients.'

'No, I won't. I want to take a break.'

The bai was shocked. 'Arrey, O sahib, there is no break in the lives of whores and pimps. We work every single day to survive. Don't you know?

He remained lying.

Her patience was running out. She felt like calling her muscleman. But she did not want to lose him. Her kotha was doing better than all the others. He was by far the best pimp around.

'You've gone mad. What'll you eat?'

'I have some money.'

'Chootia, how long will that last?'

Chhotu had become immune to abuses and insults. 'I don't know.'

'You street dog, I'll get you admitted to Shahdara mental hospital! You need treatment urgently,' she fumed.

After she had gone, he got up and went out. But he did not look for customers. Instead, he went to the Railway Goods Yard and spent the night there, lying down on a pile of bundles. But he could not sleep a wink. Mosquitoes punctured his body all over. The next morning, he slunk into the kotha. The bai saw him but she was too shrewd to escalate matters.

∽

His constant proximity to women having sex turned his desire into a raging fire. He felt heat shooting out of his ears, nostrils, and eyes. If not satiated he would burn into ashes. He felt he would lose control, drag one into a cubicle, bite into her succulent flesh, and knead her body. At other times, during the day, in his idle moments, he would fantasize about the one he fancied. She was the most attractive of the lot. Even now, occasionally she joked with him or chatted about the world outside.

One day he went out and appeared in the kotha drunk, dressed in new clothes, wearing perfume, and smoking a cigarette—instead of his usual bidi—like a Bollywood hero.

None of the women, including the bai, recognized him at first glance. But in a few seconds, they did. His favourite was busy with a customer. He walked up to the girl who wore jeans and T-shirt at night to heighten her sensuality. Her breasts and thighs showed to her advantage.

'What's all this, Chhotu?' she asked.

'He wants you, heroine!' quipped a woman. There was a collective titter.

He did not speak. He just put money in her hand—an amount double her rate—and tried to lead her towards a cubicle.

But she stood rooted to the ground. When he looked at her inquiringly, she hurled the money at his face and screamed in a shrill voice, 'Sssaale, showing me the money? Know who you are? Do you? You are a pimp...a bhadwa... yes, a bhadwa! A mangy dog surviving on our leftovers! I will not allow you to touch my body at any cost. You will contaminate it. You are dog shit! Know that?'

He stood stunned and immobile for some time and then slowly turned to leave. Suddenly, a kick landed on his butt, and he lurched towards the staircase.

He dragged himself down the steps with leaden feet and walked distraught and dazed, in the middle of the road, oblivious of the world around him.

Kallu was trailing him softly, silently.

MEGALOMANIA

JOBETH ANN WARJRI

She took the scissors from the holder. *Snip, snip, snip* and the dress material took shape. It has to have a calf-length flared skirt, a narrow waist, and broad shoulders. This is how a dress should be. She had chosen the material carefully—coral pink chiffon—that would sway in a slight gust of wind. She will have the woman down the hall try it on. Heaven knows, *she* needed to have someone tell her what to wear and how. She cannot understand how people live most of their lives without a care for how things should be. Just last night, she found a little boy flinging a sweet wrapper down the stairs. She had tsk-ed, tsk-ed at him and he promptly took to his heels wailing. Good. Someone should teach kids how to behave responsibly; except, most adults behave just as badly. This frustrated her. Imagine those thirty-somethings who drink, smoke, and did God-only-knows what else? Not her. No, siree. Those are bad habits and they are bad people. And she? She is on the right side, the truth. Never tasted wine, wrinkled her nose at the slightest whiff of smoke, and stayed away from the fornicators. Of course, sometimes it can't be helped. Sometimes she senses that she needs them in order to reassure herself that she is right. She also reasons that people could do with some sound advice from her. Like that time at the party. The wine was flowing and some of the party-goers had managed to find a guitar and were singing raucously. That was when she spotted her—poor Nyla, tugging at her blouse. Poor Nyla must have been about twenty-five, younger than her by at least ten years. Smiles were exchanged and she took her cue.

'You know, you shouldn't be wearing a sari,' she said as she sidled next to her. 'You look uncomfortable in it. I, however, am used to wearing it since I was in class eight. A dress suits you better.'

Nyla blushed. 'Well, this *is* only the third time I'm wearing one.'

'Why don't you come visit me? Lunch, tomorrow? I live on the first floor of the apartment block down the hill.'

'Sure.'

The next day, poor Nyla arrived despite the rain. The bottom of her jeans were soaking wet and she resembled a lost puppy. Just as well. Any raggedly puppy is welcome to this wolf's parlour. Poor Nyla was as raggedly as it gets. She sized her up: hands rubbing against each other (palms first, then the right hand coiled around the left thumb and, finally, ending with the left hand stroking the fingers of the right), shoulders (a bit of a slump), eyes (shifting), and mouth (eager smile). It would take some work, she knew, but the end result would be worth it.

'Have a seat,' she said pulling a chair.

'Thank you.'

'So, do you cook?'

'Not really,' replied poor Nyla apologetically. 'I can only make dal and fried veggies, sometimes egg.'

'Cooking is an art,' she said as she gently swirled the vegetable curry with a ladle. 'See, now I'm cooking this curry. First you have to heat the oil, then add the onions with garlic and ginger paste, then the spices one by one...

make sure the spices are cooked, then comes the vegetables and finally, curd.'

'That's nice,' responded poor Nyla. 'I never learnt to cook that way.'

'If you stay with me, I can teach you many things.'

From that moment on, poor Nyla became a regular visitor at her house. She learnt many things—how to brew tea the right way, how to sew buttons, even how to eat her soup. Always, there were rules that needed to be followed. For instance, tea has to be brewed for exactly two minutes; any time longer than that would leave the tea bitter and a lesser time would make it too weak. Friendship between the two women grew. Her ideas about perfection awed poor Nyla, who was always willing to please. She, for her part, was only too happy to find someone who agreed with her in most areas of life. Then, poor Nyla had done something that was outrageous.

It began rather innocuously. About a year into their friendship, she noticed a change in poor Nyla. Her hair, which was usually unkempt, began to fall in place. Poor Nyla also started wearing more skirts and dresses instead of the usual stonewashed jeans. She seemed to be paying a little more attention to her appearance: a hint of lipstick, lacquered nails, and kohl-lined eyes. At first, she attributed poor Nyla's transformation to her influence. Poor Nyla looked more 'girlish' and that must be because *she* had set an example for the younger woman to follow. Poor Nyla also started having a confident air about her. One time, she even let out a laugh. But just as she was revelling in the changes she thought was due to her, poor Nyla did something unexpected—she started making excuses for not coming to her house or for not having the time to stay on a little longer. One day, it was because poor Nyla's mother was ill; the next, because she had a dentist appointment. Then, poor Nyla declined an invitation to dinner without saying why. Her suspicions were aroused and speculation made up for what she lacked by way of evidence: poor Nyla must have a new best friend—hadn't she twitched when she reached for her hand across the dining table? Or, and even more convincing, she had fallen in love! It must be one of those good-for-nothing boys with leather jackets, always lurking about in street corners, smoking and drinking. She had read about them in a novel—*Shillong* something. It alarmed her that such characters existed. Poor Nyla needed saving and the opportunity soon presented itself.

On a fairly bright Monday in July, she spotted a familiar figure walking down the street with a middle-aged woman. She took a minute to compose herself—the meeting must appear as natural and unexpected as possible.

'Nyla dear, what a surprise! I haven't seen you for two weeks now!' she exclaimed, extending her arms to embrace poor Nyla.

She felt poor Nyla's body stiffen. No matter. She will deal with that later.

'This is my mother,' said poor Nyla, gesturing towards the woman standing next to her.

'Aunty! So good to finally meet you,' she said. 'You know, Nyla has been coming to my house often. I've been teaching her things. She's so beautiful, isn't she?"

'Thank you for your concern for her,' the woman responded.

'Not at all. I am glad for the company she gives me. If you ask me, we are like sisters now. How about you give me your number? That way, we can all meet.'

'I don't see why not,' replied poor Nyla's mother. 'It's such a wonderful thing that Nyla has someone to look out for her.'

'Oh, it's my pleasure,' she said as she took down the number. 'See you soon!'

As she made her way homewards, a plan took shape. She would have to be careful, she knew. But first, there was a meal to prepare. She took a look at her ingredients: a kilo of mutton, a kilo of fish, baingan, potatoes, carrots, tomatoes, beans, rice, and lentil. The baingan would have to be fried with turmeric and salt, she decided, while spices for the rest would have to be just right; enough to produce a tang but not to overwhelm the flavours of the meat and vegetables. Within three days, poor Nyla and her mother arrived to a feast—mutton rogan josh, fish curry, deep-fried baingan, fried vegetables with a hint of coriander, pulao, boiled rice, and dal. There were also some fresh-off-the-stove jalebis for dessert. She scanned her guests' faces and was certain that the web she had spun had caught its prey. Now onto the consumption. The plates and cutlery were laid out and the eating began.

'So, Nyla,' she started, puncturing the pulao with a ladle. 'What have you been up to these days?'

'Nothing much,' replied poor Nyla. 'I've been busy with my studies.'

'Oh, what are you planning to study? Where?' she asked, gently stirring the fish curry with another ladle.

'She's studying for a PhD entrance test,' replied poor Nyla's mother. 'We hope she will get into the university at Mawlai.'

'A lot of local boys go there, don't they?' she said. 'You have to be careful.'

A piece of mutton plonked onto poor Nyla's plate.

'Why? What have you heard?' asked poor Nyla's mother.

'I don't want to alarm you, but I've heard from some pretty reliable sources that they—the students—do drugs. I've read somewhere that one needs only hang out with the wrong crowd to get into the habit. Perhaps Nyla is different.'

'Nyla, is that true? What about your friends from the university? Do they do drugs too?' asked poor Nyla's mother, aghast. Aha! So poor Nyla *had* found new friends. Her suspicions were right all along. Back to the eating. The jalebis were out and poor Nyla was fumbling with her food: a sign of guilt?

'Well, I wouldn't know,' replied poor Nyla, after a long pause. 'I have never seen them at it.'

'Just because you haven't seen them doing it, doesn't mean they're innocent,' she remarked. 'People, especially the younger generation, can be such hypocrites. In front of you, they appear so child-like and innocent but behind your back, they're doing something else.'

She looked at poor Nyla pointedly. At this juncture, poor Nyla's face turned red—a sure sign of guilt, she reasoned.

'Are you suggesting that my Nyla too is on drugs?' asked the now distraught mother.

'Oh no, it is not my position to suggest anything,' she replied. 'But you know what they say about birds of a feather. Perhaps it is better for Nyla to get married to a nice boy from *our* community. These local boys are only out for trouble, if you know what I mean.'

Silence. She put the last piece of jalebi into her mouth. The meal was done and she had had her fill.

'I think Nyla and I should get going,' said the flustered

and confused mother. 'Thank you so much for the wonderful dinner.'

'No problem. No problem at all,' she said, a satisfied smile lighting up her face.

∽

The sewing machine ground to a halt and she snipped the last remaining thread from the material. Softly, she lifted her creation and laid it on her bed. Yes, it is a beautiful dress and the woman down the hall would be privileged to have it. She took some time to admire it and the memories came flooding back. Nyla, poor Nyla. What a pity. The dress could have been hers. Inadvertently, she winced at the thought. She had engineered it so well, and yet, it was not to be. Where could it have gone wrong? Was she too insistent? Hadn't she been exceptionally kind? She missed Nyla's company; missed the way Nyla would hang on to every word she said with those puppy-dog eyes of hers. There were other visits too when she had walked all the way to Nyla's house and kept her mother company. She had stayed away from Nyla's father when she realized that he was non-committal to her stories. The mother, too, had become wary of her visits. Pity them because she was right...*is* right. She shoved her thoughts on the matter to the back of her mind because just thinking about it made her well up in anger and frustration. She gazed at the clock on the wall: 5 p.m. She took out a sari from the cupboard—silk; cream-coloured with pink borders. A pair of matching earrings came out of the vanity case. A bit of kohl for the eyes, frost-pink lipstick and perfume behind the ears and she was ready.

She arrived at the party when the cake was being cut.

Jobeth Ann Warjri

The usual gang of fools were already there. Slowly, she took some sips of the orange juice and her eyes wandered. There he was, standing awkwardly at the far end of the room. She smiled in his direction.

THE PATIENT
SOURABH MUKHERJEE

I looked up from my phone as the next patient walked in. He appeared to be in his thirties. He was tall and slim with square jaws and expressive eyes. The unruly mop of hair added to his somewhat boyish charm. His stubble was a couple of days old. He wore a pair of jeans, which had seen better days, and a full-sleeve shirt with the sleeves rolled up.

He walked in gingerly and stood still a few inches from my table. He looked around, his eyes narrowed in suspicion, as if there were others in the room watching him. In reality, it was just the two of us inside my chamber that Saturday afternoon.

I gestured at the chair across the table, urging him to sit down.

'Make yourself comfortable,' I smiled reassuringly at the young man. 'What should I call you?'

He kept looking around the room, averting my eyes, as he sat down.

'Ashu.... Ashutosh...my name is Ashutosh,' he said hesitatingly.

'Tell me, Ashutosh, how can I help you?' I said disarmingly.

His eyes were now cast downwards, his fingers on my table twitched anxiously. He remained silent for a few minutes, and then spoke suddenly, 'Your receptionist... Mrs Roy...is a very nice person. Had it not been for her, I wouldn't have managed to see you. I didn't have an appointment, you see. You are a successful psychiatrist... and quite famous...'

'Thank you so much for your kind words, Ashutosh,' I did not let him finish, 'I'm just another human being like yourself trying to help others.... I do not have extraordinary powers....'

Ashutosh was now nervously drumming on the tabletop. His eyes still downcast, he spoke almost in whispers, 'You are being too modest, Doctor... I've... I've heard a lot about you...your successes...almost miraculous.... Mrs Roy has told me wonderful things about you...you have saved lives; you have brought people back from the brink of destruction....'

I smiled and said, 'It's too kind of Mrs Roy, but I don't think so myself, Ashutosh. Each one of us has the strength within. I can only help you figure out where the problem really lies, and then help you find a way to fix it.'

Ashutosh suddenly looked up and locked his eyes with mine.

'That's strange! That's not what I expected when I came here! I will pay you your fees only to hear that I'll have to fix my own problem? That's not fair! Not fair at all!' he paused briefly and said, 'Everyone thinks it's easy to take me for a ride!'

I kept looking at Ashutosh, letting the moment pass. I did not want to react to his perception about the discipline of psychiatry. After a few seconds, I asked him, 'Ashutosh, what makes you think that you've been taken for a ride?'

Ashutosh kept looking at me, his brows wrinkled. He did not answer my question.

'Ashutosh, I won't be able to help you, if you don't trust me,' I tried to sound firm.

'Actually, I don't think you can help me...nobody can....' Ashutosh whispered, sounding somewhat restless, 'I know I'm the one at fault....'

'Ashutosh, why don't we talk about it?' I bent forward on the table.

'You know what, Doctor? I'm scared...very scared....' his lips trembled, 'unless someone or something stops me, I may end up doing something very wrong!'

'What do you mean, Ashutosh?' I was very curious.

Ashutosh clenched his fists so tightly that he almost broke the skin of his palms. He took a deep breath and said, 'With these hands...with these very hands.... I do things that make me hate myself....'

'There's a beast lurking inside each one of us, Ashutosh! Don't beat yourself up for that. It can always be tamed. Now, tell me what you've done.'

'I feel attracted to others' stuff....' his face was dark. His eyes were again cast downwards. He continued, 'I've stolen *stuff*....'

'What kinds of *stuff*?' I asked, stressing on the last word. The things we steal often tell a lot about us.

'Women's clothing...undergarments...of beautiful women. *She* was very beautiful too, you know....' Ashutosh was looking away from me, his voice reduced to murmurs.

'*She*...the one who you think took you for a ride?'

Ashutosh nodded.

'Do you realize that, stealing is the first step towards complete moral degradation?'

He nodded again.

'Tell me, Ashutosh...do you regret your actions afterwards?'

'I do, please believe me...I hate myself...but I feel the urge...an almost compulsive urge to discover her smell...you see, I've been hurt...very badly.' When he looked into my eyes again, I saw that his eyes were moist.

I smiled and said, 'Hurt! That's something all of us share, don't we? Haven't we all been hurt at some moment or the other in this unpredictable journey of life? Let me tell you about myself.'

Ashutosh sat up straight. He was finally focusing, for the first time since he had walked into my chamber. This always works!

'Ashutosh, I come from this really small village near Burdwan. When I cleared my medical entrance examinations, I had to leave my village and shift to Kolkata for my studies. There was this girl in my village whom I loved with all my heart. Her name was Anjana, I used to call her Anju. We'd been together right from high school. I had to stay away from Anju when I moved to Kolkata for my studies. In the lonely nights inside my small room, which I shared with another boy in the hostel, I stayed awake and comforted myself by remembering the promises we had made to each other. Turned out, those promises meant nothing to her. She went ahead and married the first man her father had chosen for her. A businessman with money to throw around, who would keep her happy. She didn't even bother to inform me! I came to know when I visited my village during the Pujas.... I had brought gifts for her, can you believe it? But she had already left our village with her husband....'

I stopped when I realized that my eyes had welled up. I did not have to cook that story up, and the tears came easily that Saturday afternoon.

The Patient

'So, what did you do?' Ashutosh asked, looking anxious, running his fingers through his hair.

'Nothing,' I tried to smile, 'love, so intense and all-consuming, happens only once in a lifetime. I've been alone since then, living with Anju's memories.'

Ashutosh suddenly stood up, shaking his head. He was again restless.

'Yes...you've been betrayed too! You are no better than me! Listen, I won't waste any more of your time.... I'll try to "fix this myself"...just as you said...and if I can't, I'll come back to you,' he said, looking away from me, as he headed for the door.

He pushed the door open and stepped out. The door closed behind him.

A few minutes later, the door opened again.

It was my receptionist, Anjali. She had started working for me about a year back. She was in her mid-twenties. She was gentle in her manners and efficient at her work. With her kohl-rimmed eyes, sharp features, hair cascading down past her shoulders, and an immaculately maintained physique, I was sure she was quite used to second glances.

'Sir, Mr Chowdhury wants you to visit him in the morning tomorrow. I've checked your appointments. You have a light morning tomorrow.'

'Did he call?' I asked her. Her lavender perfume wafted inside my chamber.

'He did, sir.'

'Okay, call him back and tell him I'll be there.'

Anjali nodded and headed for the door.

'Anyone else waiting outside?' I asked her.

'Yes, sir', Anjali smiled, 'there are two more patients waiting outside, in fact.'

'The last one, for some reason, got me completely exhausted,' my fingers went to my temples. I had a throbbing headache.

'Sir, I've been warning you,' Anjali walked up to my table and smiled warmly, 'you are working too hard. Let me get you your pills.'

Anjali went out and came back with a couple of Crocin tablets and a glass of water. Anjali was caring, almost maternal at times, and that quality of hers never failed to touch me deeply.

When I finished the water, and handed the empty glass back to her, Anjali said, 'Sir, I'm planning to leave a bit early today, if that's okay with you....'

'May I ask why,' I smiled.

'Well...Mohit and I are planning to spend the evening together...it's our—'

'Let me guess!' I did not let her finish, 'Your wedding anniversary, isn't it? A year already?'

'Not really,' Anjali laughed, 'it's been six months! It probably sounds stupid, but Mohit insisted that we celebrate. He feels that making a marriage work for six months isn't easy these days!'

'He's right,' I laughed out loudly. 'How many relationships actually work these days?'

I was beginning to feel a weight on my chest. The betrayal that Ashutosh had been subjected to, and the pain that had been eating away into his soul, slowly turning him into a delinquent, had somehow managed to scrape my own wound—a wound that was not to be soothed that afternoon with stories of successful six-month-old marriages.

The Patient

I had thought that Ashutosh would not come again. But he did, the very next Saturday. At the same time.

His clothes were rumpled, his hair was a mess. He was carrying a bag.

He walked up to my table and placed the bag on it. He then sat on the chair across my table.

'Your receptionist, Mrs Roy, is most kind. I don't know what I'd do without her....'

I looked into his eyes and asked, 'How are you, Ashutosh? And what's in that bag?'

'I'm not well, Doctor,' he bent forward and whispered, his voice shaking, 'please help me!'

'I *will* help you, Ashutosh. Tell me what's going on.'

'Open that bag, Doctor. You will know.'

As I opened the bag, a heady aroma, distinctly feminine, filled the air in the room. Inside the bag were neatly arranged clothes, all belonging to women. Saris, salwar suits, office-wear, party dresses, night-wear, skirts, ladies' trousers and jeans, and undergarments. I looked up at Ashutosh, my mouth gaping.

'I can sense the poison running through my veins, Doctor, and it's killing me,' Ashutosh began to weep, 'I can't control my urges any more. I'm going around stealing these...at nights, mostly...but I can't, for God's sake, find her smell... will you ever be able to cure me?'

'Of course, you'll be fine, Ashutosh,' I cleared out my table, putting everything back inside the bag and smiled at him warmly. 'You will need to get a grip on yourself. You need to tell yourself constantly that you wouldn't destroy yourself, just because someone hurt you.'

Ashutosh bent forward and took my hands in his.

'That's the very reason why I'm here, Doctor. Help me... please help me. Look inside that bag, and you will find the addresses of the houses from where I've stolen these things. Will you please send these things back to the women they belong to? I...I promise I won't do this ever again....'

I nodded, though, I knew that I would never do what Ashutosh had wanted me to. There would be too many doubts, too many questions.

I kept the bag away inside a cupboard in my chamber. Ashutosh stood up and left as abruptly as he had come in.

∽

It was not too long before Anjali found that bag.

A couple of days later, as soon as I walked into my chamber in the morning, Anjali asked me, 'Sir, there's a bag in your cupboard. I was getting the room cleaned and found it. I...I'm sorry, I opened it. I was curious....' Shock was writ large on Anjali's face.

'Have a seat,' I gestured at the chair across my table. Anjali sat down, and I told her everything about my patient. I did not mention his name, as my professional ethics forbade me to.

When I finished, Anjali looked listlessly outside the window. 'A man, betrayed in love, hunting for the smell of his beloved...and as he hurtles down the path of self-destruction, his inner conflict is killing him. He is a seriously flawed man, but I feel for him....'

Anjali had tears in her eyes. And at that moment, I liked her more than I ever had.

∽

A couple of weeks passed by. I was certain that Ashutosh would not return. He had probably managed to get a grip on his fantastic urges.

The Patient

But I was soon proven wrong.

That was a busy morning, and I had just finished talking to a patient. I was about to press the bell and instruct Anjali to send in the next patient, when Ashutosh stormed into my room, dishevelled and restless as usual.

He occupied the chair across my table, and bent forward, his mouth inches from my face.

'Doctor, I seriously need your help...this is going from bad to worse....'

'What's it now?'

'Look, I...I've got myself binoculars...and these days, all I'm doing is snooping on women...beautiful women... like *her*....'

'So, you're now a stalker?' I didn't let Ashutosh finish.

'You can call me anything...but I need your help...I haven't slept for nights...I keep watching women...in kitchens making dinner...in bedrooms changing clothes...sometimes in washrooms if I manage to—'

I raised my hand to stop him.

'Ashutosh, you'd get yourself into serious trouble one of these days,' I warned him, but Ashutosh did not stop. What he said next made my jaw drop.

'I've been following Mrs Roy...the girl in the reception, you know...in the evenings...in the nights....'

'Ashutosh! Do you even know what you're saying? Anjali is married, for God's sake! She has a loving husband! They are a happy couple. I would suggest you stay away from them! This is an order!'

Ashutosh grabbed my hands. 'I can't live without her, Doctor! I need her...please! Please help me....'

'Ashutosh, you're losing it!'

He did not relent. 'I need her, Doctor. I've fallen in love

with her…and only you can help me!'

'There are plenty of nice women around, Ashutosh. Find someone and settle down. You'll find peace. You'll be happy,' I tried to dissuade him.

'That's not possible, Doctor. I want to be with her…do you think I should speak to her?'

'Listen Ashutosh, don't even dream of doing that! Leave her alone!'

Ashutosh suddenly moved back and reclined on the chair. His face was contorted in his hatred for me. 'I get it. I get it, Doctor! You don't want to cure me. Here I am, freaking out, and you're enjoying this, lecturing me on morals! Shove those morals up your—'

'Enough!' I raised my hand. 'Calm down, Ashutosh. Get a grip on yourself. Don't let that animal out.' I tried to calm him down.

But, Ashutosh would not listen to me. He stood up, kicking the chair back, and stormed out of the room.

I was angry, almost shaking. I was also worried for Anjali.

For a fleeting second, I wondered if I should inform the police.

I dialled the number. I heard the voice at the other end. Then, I ended the call.

Maybe I should speak to Ashutosh one more time. There was no point handing a sick man over to the police.

I knew Ashutosh would be back.

∽

The next morning, when I walked into my chamber, I saw Anjali sitting at the reception with a grim face. Her eyes were red, and it did not look like she had slept well.

The Patient

I walked up to her and asked, 'Anjali, is everything fine?'

'Sir, can we talk inside your chamber for a few minutes?' She looked around. There were a couple of patients waiting.

'Of course, come in,' I stepped aside and let Anjali walk in to my chamber.

Once inside, I shut the door behind us.

'What's the matter, Anjali? You look upset!'

'Sir, I had the most dreadful night,' she unlocked her phone and inched closer.

She went to her message inbox and pointed to a number.

There were forty-seven messages from that number.

'Sir, someone kept sending me these messages all through the night! Mohit and I called the number, but he wouldn't pick up. And this went on and on. Mohit and I ended up having a fight. He now feels that I know this man...that I'm having an affair with him!' Anjali broke down.

'Anjali, listen to me. Calm down!' I steadied her by her shoulders. 'Take the day off and go home. I'll talk to Mohit. He's a nice guy, he'll understand....'

'Thank you so much, sir. I genuinely need some rest....'

As Anjali walked out of my room, I ran my fingers through my hair and sighed.

I could guess who had sent her those messages all through the night.

Ashutosh!

∽

Ashutosh stormed into my chamber the following Saturday afternoon. I had met all my patients and was about to wind up for the day.

I looked into his eyes and said, 'Ashutosh, we need to talk. What do you think you are up to?'

Ashutosh did not sit. Nor did he bother to reply.

He kept rubbing his hands, and said, 'Doctor, do you remember that you had told me to fix my problem all by myself? Well, here's the good news! I have fixed my problem. I don't think I'll need to bother you ever again.'

'Well, congratulations, Ashutosh. I'm curious to know how you've sorted yourself out....'

'I've decided to marry Anjali. I'll be a different man. All my demons will be dealt with. I won't need your help again, Doctor!'

'Ashutosh, take a seat. We need to talk. You need to stop bothering her—'

'Shut up! Shut the fuck up, Doctor!' Ashutosh did not let me finish and screamed, 'I'm not here to listen to your lectures on what's right and what's not. I've expressed my feelings for her. She hasn't turned me down. Which means only one thing—she loves me too. You dare not get in our way, Doctor! Now, call her!'

I felt helpless. 'Ashutosh, you aren't leaving me any other option. I'll need to call the police!'

'You think you'll scare me away, do you? I want to live, Doctor. Whatever it takes....'

Suddenly, he rushed towards my table and pressed the bell, before I could stop him.

It was too late. The noise seemed to reverberate through the room.

A few seconds passed.

Anjali walked into my room.

'Yes, sir?' she smiled tentatively. She must have heard our loud voices, already.

Ashutosh shoved me aside and stood in front of her.

'Anju!' he looked into her eyes.

The Patient

Anjali was taken aback.

'Anju,' Ashutosh repeated, 'I can't take this sweet torture any more!'

Ashutosh held her by her arms.

'What do you think you're trying to do?' Anjali tried to free herself, her face flushed in rage.

'Believe me, Anju! I can't live without you...I'm lonely, I'm lost...it's up to you now to save me from myself...please....'

'Are you out of your mind?' Anjali finally managed to free herself and turned around, almost running towards the door.

Ashutosh lunged forward and grabbed a corner of her pallu.

'How dare you run away from me? From *me*? From the man who loves you madly....' Ashutosh screamed.

'You are sick...you need help....' Anjali tried to free her sari from the clutches of the monster.

The beast inside was unleashed. Ashutosh came under the grip of unbridled rage.

His hands circled around Anjali's neck.

'What...what are you doing?' Anjali managed to mutter, almost choking.

'I've suffered enough...I've been lonely for years! No one rejects me ever again...no one! Did you hear that? I've died every single moment through these years.... I won't let *you* live happily after destroying me, my dreams!'

Ashutosh's fingers sank deeper into Anjali's neck. Her hands flailed helplessly, and her eyes almost popped out, as she struggled for one last breath.

'Sir, sir...why...why are you doing this to me....'

Those were Anjali's last words. She collapsed like a rag doll on the carpet.

I came back to my senses. Anjali's last words seemed to echo around the room.

'Sir, sir...why...why are you doing this to me....'

Why did she call me in her final moments? That question should have been directed to Ashutosh!

I looked around the closed room.

There was no one—just me and the lifeless body of Anjali on the carpet. There was no trace of Ashutosh. That was my bag filled with women's garments that I had stolen and hidden inside that cupboard. You would also find a pair of binoculars inside my briefcase, and a SIM card hidden carefully inside my wallet, to be used only during the night when Ashutosh wanted to express his love for Anju...Anjali...Anjana.... The names got muddled up in my brain. They were all the same, none of them loved me. I looked once again at the body on the carpet.

I wondered what Ashutosh would have to say about that, the next time he visited me.

THE TENANT

RACHITA RAJ

The moon sat suspended low in the night sky, fat and bulging, like a luminescent orange-grey egg yolk. I leaned back against the pillow and looked around the room. Dull walls of an indeterminate colour stared wanly back at me, a heap of flaky paint-plaster in a corner where the rainwater had seeped in, moths dancing dangerously around a naked bulb. I sighed, satisfied, lying easily in my favourite blanket, and allowed myself a brief smile.

It was the end of week one in the new flat. My last landlord's wife had caught him in bed with the maid and thrown him out, bringing my tenancy to a swift and abrupt end. Broker John, real-estate agent extraordinaire, had come gallantly to my rescue and found me this gem: a little third-floor flat in a quiet back-lane of a leafy old neighbourhood. 'The landlords are an elderly couple and live on the ground floor. Bade non-interfering hain, aur flat ka separate entrance bhi hai. The rent is low.'

My antenna had tingled for an instant, heart beating with a twinge of hesitation: *How did the house just happen to be empty? Who had moved away? Why was the rent so low? Why doesn't anyone live on the first two floors? Whatever, maybe the owners are nitpicky about whom they rent to. Good thing I am such a good girl.*

I had somehow convinced myself thus and moved in

immediately with my meagre belongings: the frames on the wall (Nicholas Roerich Himalayan sweeps and inky-charcoal Gond art on parchment paper), a giant hotel-quality mattress (the only thing I had splurged on in this new city, my only piece of furniture, really), toiletries, and sundry household items and, finally, Alexa, my brand-new Amazon speaker thingamajig. I don't have much. I'm low-key like that. Music and rest for my bad back are all I need.

I just moved here to this bustling metroscape from sleepy Coonoor, eager to escape the well-meaning yet cloying arms of my protective parents (I am an only child and have rendered them empty-nesters). I am a hermit, in my own head all the time, used to staring out of the window at misty mountains, cocooned in Led Zeppelin and Middle Earth reveries.

But I realized I *had* to get out in the real world. And to effectively assimilate (and not be scared by) this new physical space that I had consciously thrust myself into, I decided that I needed to temper my excursions out. I had convinced myself that nifty little Alexa was my buffer—till I was ready.

My new colleagues are nice but I demur at their invitations for after-work drinks at the nearby bar, preferring, instead, my solitude. And Alexa. Music has been my refuge and harbour in the stormy seas of anxiety and social interaction. I have ploughed through bulky Sony Discmans in my adolescence, iPods, and cheaper MP3 players, all in a quest to drown out the voices in my head telling me I should go out more. Music is all I need, man. And, now, with Alexa in the picture, it is easier than ever.

Alexa sings from day to night, blaring strains of this and that, transporting me aurally through small towns and

The Tenant

cities and seas and prairies and moonland—Springsteen and Cohen and Joni and Björk and Bowie. Themes of freedom and escaping small-town mind-numbness course through my brain.

I worry the neighbours will complain about the ceaseless walls of sound that stand guard for me and disrupt the night air. But then I remember I'm the only tenant. Everyone on the two floors below mysteriously moved out a month ago. The twinge in my heart again, heartbeat quickening. *Why?* White noise plugs my ears for a nanosecond but Björk's eerie melody resounds: *I've seen it all / I have seen the trees / I have seen the willow leaves / Dancing in the breeze.*

Jesus, I am getting the creeps. The hair on the back of my neck rising and gooseflesh appearing spontaneously on my arms. *Cigarette peete hain, fuck this.* I grab my smokes and light and swing the door open to the terrace, all mine.

I can see the tops of trees and other houses, their rain-mottled walls looking weird and veiny in the streetlamp light, but it's OK, it's the monsoons—which have gone on forever now, fuck. I am grateful for this place, though, in spite of its singular dinginess. It's close to work, autos are easily available and, most importantly, it was there when I needed it. And life goes on. I can hear Björk continue, a little muffled: *I've seen a man killed / By his best friend / And lives that were over / Before they were spent.*

Thank God, Alexa is working better now. Ever since I moved in, I sensed her being a little off: voltage fluctuations, maybe? Do speakers even get affected by stuff like that? But this is a ratty little room on the top floor, probably faulty old wiring gluing the circuits together. See, this seemed to be an ancient house, falling apart at the seams, so I figured it had something to do with that. The bad-voltage juju must have fried the WiFi and thus Alexa. Because she even started switching off, man. At least I had to tell myself that to feel better.

I even checked with the old landlord couple, who said their electrical appliances were working OK. But that aunty looked shifty. Maybe it's the squint in her eye and sour smile. Anyway, but then the music started getting switched up. Randomly started playing different songs. Ghazals start playing. Shit I *never* hear otherwise. *Aaj jaane ki zidd na karo.* Farida Khanum's voice, mellifluous but unwelcome, clashed like angry cymbals in my confused head the first time. And then, immediately after, there was this weird cackling... *laugh*? Was that fear that made me gasp and flinch at the sound, like a physical blow to my back? BS. I decided to pooh-pooh the feeling away. *This bloody Alexa is just being a creeper. Come on, ya, Alexa, don't be a bitch now,* I had said aloud, feeling foolish at my initial fright.

But I hadn't slept a wink that night.

I had obviously turned to the Internet gods to quell my fears. Whew. Hundreds of people worldwide were facing this issue too—Reddit threads that extended for miles! Hallelujah! Amazon had issued an official advisory to the Alexa owners: *Yes, there have been a few instances but we are acknowledging it as a bug in the AI, a technical glitch. A hard reset will fix everything. There is no cause for worry.* I'm soothed by the answer, at least there's an explanation for it.

Whew at least I will rest well tonight. I've not been sleeping fitfully ever since I moved in. I wake up exhausted and nervous from dreams too fuzzy to remember. It's like I've been running marathons or brawling with invisible foes while asleep. I've pegged it to moving stress and no alcohol on account of being too busy. I will fix this tomorrow—it is Friday. I'm done with my smoke now and flick the cigarette butt into the distance. The screen door slams shut behind me as I walk into my humble digs. Alexa, glowing grey-white, occupies a pride of place on my still-unarranged mountain of books. I have unplugged her completely and will be leaving her off for the night. Let her rest a little. And me too.

Silvery moonbeams are seeping in from a giant window, the only feature of note in the room. I have not yet bought new curtains to fit its frame. Alexa glistens, almost rippling like water in the stillness. I shudder for no reason. Shaking my head, punctuating it with a nervous laugh, to make myself feel brave, even brazen, I grab the garbage bag and head downstairs to keep it out for the koodawallah's visit the next morning.

On my way back to the flat, I pass Tinku, the maid's child, on the stairwell. A quiet little thing with bulging eyes.

'Didi ko hello bolna,' he says.

'Kaun didi?'

'Woh didi jo yahaan aapke pehle rehti thi.'

'OK bye, ha, kal milte hain,' I stutter and bolt up the stairs, running the rest of the way up.

What a weird fucking child, dude. Damn.

I walk back in and secure the door behind me. Tinku's words have unsettled me. My heart is quivering again. What did the landlords say when I casually asked them who lived here last, before me? They had stuttered and ummed and aahed and said there was a girl who left overnight. *We don't know why.*

I had even sauntered over to Tinku and obliquely put questions to him: *Who was she? When did she leave?* When questioned about said didi's whereabouts, bug-eyed Tinku gets evasive and tells me, eyes darting around like a hunted animal, that he doesn't know, that she left suddenly one day. 'Bas unko puraane gaane bade pasand the.'

Why, though? I contemplate, looking again at the same fat moon, grey and morose.

I can see myself in the humongous glass window, dull bulb glowering faintly on, Alexa behind me, and my beloved mattress-bed too.

There's suddenly some movement, a reflection, a dash of wispy black cloud, I can't really tell. My stomach plummets to my shoes and I dart around, heart beating in my ears.

Nothing. There's nothing. Hahaha. God, what a scare. I should go to bed, bury myself in my blankets, emerge only in the safety of daylight.

I grab my phone and start walking towards my phone charger, when music pierces the night quiet.

Aaj jaane ki zidd na karo.

Silence. Five long seconds. Nothing. And then the laughter again.

∽

Brutal suicide shocks residents
11/06/2019
According to police, a young woman living on the third floor of a residential complex in Anand Nagar allegedly committed suicide late last night. An out-of-towner who had only moved in a week ago, she jumped to her death through a large window in her room, pummelling through it like a bull. Investigations are ongoing.

WHEN THE SUN FALLS FROM THE SKY
ANURADHA VIJAYAKRISHNAN

However hot the day has been, our sun is always the same shade of orange in the evening. Orange and belly round—in that same nook of sky where it stood yesterday. Every evening I look up and it is there, and it makes me certain of everything else around me in our home, our town which is the only town I know, and everywhere beyond.

Sometimes I dream of how the sun might fall to the ground one day like an overripe mango or a dead old guardian-warrior, and how the crows come swooping down for it, black talons out. How mother crows yank out the dripping, rosy, entrails, squawking in delight to young ones waiting on the branches above. How they all then feed on our sun, in the dark—how happy they are.

I have dreams of this kind and I know some dreams turn real. Amma says it is fine to dream any good dream you want as long you work *hard, hard, hard*. She has a list of these things she regularly recites to us. As if that is all she can afford to give us as we get older—strings and strings of good, shiny advice she has collected and hoarded for the sake of her daughters, like other women save jewellery. As if she is worried that even this will not be enough between her two girls. So she listens very carefully when I talk to her about anything, even if she is busy with one of the hundred chores she is always busy with. Like letting out the hem of Charu's nightdress one last time before she needs another one or checking my test papers with a meticulous eye or writing out pages and pages of accounts for the day, week, month. She listens and then replies with care as she works, always, even when I do not actually need her to say anything. Though I have never told her how I keep dreaming about the sun falling down and the world going blind, a world filled with scavenging crows.

'A thousand rupees more?' Mother's eyes send out sparks; bits of orange evening light float in them making her look pretty though she is not really a pretty woman. She is thin, pale, and sour with a permanent crease down her forehead that does not smoothen even when she smiles at us early in the morning when we are all still sleepy and soft.

'Did you really say one thousand? More?'

Charu and I continue to sip our tea huddling in the cool shadows inside the humid kitchen, picking silently at idlis left from breakfast, watching daylight ebb out of the room and evening deepen, tick-by-precise-tick of the old grandfather clock in the passage outside.

'That is just too much, my dear, Mani! You also know that.'

Mani's eyebrows fly up like a pair of scheming crows. Ssss...we hear the rustle of black wings beyond the window as birds plunge into the mango tree's cavernous body in search of nests left behind in the morning. Of course, the wings might be any colour—brown, green, blue, or yellow. Strangely enough even kingfishers live in that mango tree though there are no rivers or canals nearby! The crows are the most powerful of them all though, unafraid of the sun's big hot light.

'One thousand? God, no way, Mani! Can't give you that much....'

Amma sucks in her narrow cheeks to make her point but Mani is shaking her head vigorously. She moans, 'Ente Chechi...need the money so badly...school fees, rent....'

We push away our plates and I take another finger-lick of the chutney. The chutney is from the fridge and is cold and thick, but tastes nice and chilli-hot if I avoid the slightly burnt mustard seeds. Amma is not a bad cook but she cooks quickly. Steaming up idlis on one burner and seasoning chutney on high flame on another, with a machine load of dirty uniforms and towels chug-chugging in the background. That washing machine is older than me, bought when there was a little more money and less to spend on. The clothes come out soggy and barely clean these days. And Amma's idlis turn up moist and sticky while she shoves the overdone chutney quickly into a little steel bowl, all at the same time, every day. So she can dash into our room and help Charu get ready while shouting at me to go and have my bath, *please*.

'What can I do, Chechi...there's no one else for me, you have to help!'

We know Mani is being clever as ever. We linger, waiting for more even though it is getting late and there is homework to start. It is true she has no one else—who does? We don't, do we—but we also know she is clever, very clever. We know she steals milk packets from the milk booth on her way home in the evening. She gets away with it because the chap who runs the booth is always drunk and can't count too well.

'Hmm, so what I can do...Mani? Charu has her annual day this month. You know how much her costume cost me? Do you have any idea, aanh?'

I look at my sister and we don't know whether to smile, make faces or look away. Charu has very long hair and because of that, I am sure, they have made her the princess in the play the junior section is doing. She gets to wear a pretty red-and-gold dress and flashy, long earrings that hurt her ears but look nice. She even gets to do a tiny dance in one scene. She has to stay for practice daily after school and I go and sit there with her, reading my library book and watching her learn to walk and act like a princess which she is getting to be rather good at now. Then we cycle back home and Amma gives us tea and idlis. Though some days it is bread and jam instead. I am not sure if I like that better. The bread we buy is usually dry from having sat in the store for too long. I know the school made Amma pay for the red dress and maybe the earrings too.

'And Soma will need coaching for her finals. All these expenses, Mani! I myself could do with an extra thousand or two this month....'

Her voice loses its argumentative tone, wavers a little and suddenly we both know we are eavesdropping. So we start clearing up.

'Som-echi, what do I do with these idlis?' asks my little sister Charu, swinging her long braids from side to side and watching them go on swinging. It is the princess thing. She doesn't stop acting like one these days, even when home, especially when Amma isn't around. Walks slower, moves her head up and down in funny ways when she talks to me and keeps trying to make her pigtails dance, as if gold and pearl chains are strung on them. It is all right to dream, as Amma says, but this was getting silly, wasn't it?

'Back in the fridge, silly! Isn't that what we do every day? Can't waste them!' I answer her curtly. I begin to wipe the table as she stands on tiptoe and carefully starts rinsing plates and glasses.

Mani comes in the evening and sweep-mops the house in a whirlwind in one hour, rushing around the house holding the long-handled broom up at an odd angle like it were a gun and she a badly trained terrorist in a hurry. Really! Leaves soapy footmarks wherever she goes and wipes them clean only when Amma yells at her. She folds the washing, potters around a bit, then settles down in the backyard to black tea, idlis, and some conversation while Amma kneads the chapatti dough for dinner or works the day's knots slowly out of her thinning but long hair. Mani is a luxury we can barely afford, just like ice creams once a month on a Sunday evening or taking a taxi instead of the bus for trips into town. Yet Amma has kept her all these years. If she hadn't, we would have stuck out terribly in this neighbourhood as the only house without a maid. Almost every month around this time, Mani tries to talk some 'extra' out of Amma. Some months she gets it too, and the next Sunday Charu and I manage to get ice cream money out of Amma.

'Three-months' rent left to pay, Chechi...the landlord came last night...thank god my girls had the good sense not to come out....'

'Had to run and get the bastard two pots of good toddy from Kanaran's shop to make him go...he was already drunk and my daughters were at home alone...he'll come again tomorrow...Daivame, what a fate!'

Mani ends on a loud sigh and wipes her face with the end of her sari. The birds in the mango tree are quiet. They have either found their homes and children safe or flown away in despair. A glass slips from Charu's hand and Amma turns around quickly.

'Soma...what...what are you both still doing in the kitchen?'

'Nothing, Amma, just putting everything back,' she knows we were listening.

Charu and I glare at each other in order to split the guilt evenly, before I turn to switch on the kitchen light. It is very dark inside here now, but Charu comes from behind me and reaches up to switch it off.

'Electricity bills....' she mouths dramatically, sounding more like Mani than a princess soon to be crowned in a play.

Her eyes are round and black with pale kajal smudges around them. Now that she is going to be a princess, Amma lets Charu wear a bit of kajal to school. Dreaming is fine, she tells us some mornings, her palms patting our heads briefly before we run to put on our school shoes. Amma can be soft and smiling for tiny bits of time on some days, days she wakes up a bit lighter, a bit more hopeful. She has stitched an armful of sparkling sequins on Charu's scarf that she will drape around her waist in the play. She works on it in the afternoon when the light is strong in the bedroom, a cup of strong tea by her side and glasses resting on her nose. Before the children from the evening batches start arriving. Once they come, Amma gets no time for anything else and that is another reason why she rushes around in the kitchen and messes up the cooking most days. That is why we eat the same food in the morning and evening, why she actually needs Mani to come and help her with housework.

'Ey, Princess, go and wash your face,' I order Charu. She points her chin meaningfully at Amma and Mani outside, and then ambles out slowly, swinging her hips half like a dance. I watch her go. She is still a child and Amma tells her nothing. She doesn't tell me much either but sometimes

When the Sun Falls from the Sky

I think she lets me find out certain things. The other day I found bills and letters scattered on the table. All the letters were for Amma and one of them was about a loan from a bank and how two instalments were 'overdue' now. Another time, she told me that we couldn't buy a laptop this year too because we couldn't get another loan just now. I am decent at Computer Studies and usually top my class. I like Mathematics too, and History and end up doing most of Charu's homework for her. I can manage without a laptop at home but it would have been nice to have one. Really nice!

I watch Charu walk her new, dreamy walk out of the kitchen and into our bedroom. I watch her thick braids bounce prettily around her plump shape.

'Let me see. Next week, maybe, or two weeks later, OK? And I'll need it back this time.' Amma is talking to her as if Mani is her friend, as if she is not sick and tired of that woman and her constant whining and begging. Amma can be like that too, we all know....

Two weeks? I know that one lot of tuition fees will come in by then but there is usually nothing left from that after Amma has done her accounts.

Amma takes tuitions, mornings and evenings, seven days a week. She teaches young children Mathematics, English, and Physics. Some college girls from the neighbourhood too come to her for help with English. Amma has a good name as a teacher. She used to be a good student, is a determined teacher, and keeps her fees low. So, there's never been any trouble getting students. Right now, she teaches four batches daily with over a dozen kids in each batch. The college girls come on weekends and for them Amma puts on her spectacles and takes out books from the glass cupboard in her room. I help her put them back but have never read any of them. Some evenings, she gets hoarse with all the shouting at children who are not as smart as we—Charu and I—are, but still pay our mother good money. Hoarse and prickly. We hate our mother then; hate the way she snaps at us if we even go near her. Then I make tea and let Amma rest quietly for some time while we do the homework and light the puja lamp at dusk.

Charu doesn't like Amma teaching other children, especially the younger ones who come from schools we would never get to go to, schools with ridiculous westernized names and uniforms shorter and brighter than ours. She says it makes our mother tired and angry because those girls are so hard to teach, but she doesn't really know yet how much we need all the money our mother can make.

'Chechi, I don't want to trouble you...just give me a hundred tomorrow and I'll pay the landlord next week. Give me the rest when you get your tuition money. I'll manage till then. I have asked others too, but they are not kind like you, are they?'

'They don't know how things can get, like you and I know, do they, Chechi?'

Mani says this so softly that I have to strain to catch her words before they trail away. I am standing behind the door now, my back pressed into rough plaster that will leave tell-tale patches of grey-white on my dress. Amma will kill me if she sees me listening to their conversation and wasting my time too, but inside the dark kitchen, it feels comfortable. I sniff at the familiar smells that come from all its four familiar corners—cold tea, cheap detergent, onion peel, the waste bin, damp washcloths that will dry overnight on the towel rack where I have hung them out. Standing this way, I can see them both. Amma in profile, picking up a steel plate to cover the dough she has finished with; Mani squatting on the steps, one hand toying with the end of her pallu.

Mani is thin, even thinner than Amma, and even taller, with a long neck and a strange, manly voice that she can crack like a bullock-cart driver's whip if she is in the mood. She works in four houses and doesn't get home before seven at night. I know this because she keeps repeating all this when she chats with Amma in the evening. She tells Amma everything; she told Amma that she steals a couple of milk packets every other day and sells them cheap to her neighbours. Amma doesn't answer her immediately now. She is standing very straight and looking into some calm, distant place. She crosses and uncrosses her arms; I can see the straight line of her nose pointed proudly into the air. People say I have her nose and will turn out as tall too, though Charu has her hair. Charu will be the pretty one.

'And what if he comes again tonight, or tomorrow, Mani? What will you do? What about your girls?'

I wonder if she is mocking Mani but her tone is serious. Her hands play with the vessel of chapatti dough, spinning it this way and that way.

'The landlord, Chechi? I'll try managing him. He is greedy but a fool. One more bottle, maybe some top-class arrack from that bootlegger Vaattu Gopalan this time.... I will pour it out myself for him...hehehe...and under my pillow there's a long knife I sharpen every night...he knows that, he sure does....'

Amma laughs...a small dry sound you could mistake for a cough if you did not know her well. The mention of that knife is a joke between them. In reality, there is probably no knife, not even a rusted one. In reality, Mani might, one day, give away one of her daughters to the landlord in return for five years' rent spared. I have heard Mani herself say this, jokingly.

'The girls...be careful, Mani. They are....'

Amma is leaning against the wall, one flour-flecked palm on the door jamb. When I try to keep my eyes on her, her thick dark shadow hides her from me. Mani seems to consider what she's just heard. She stares at the ground before looking up briefly at the sky, at that orange sun that will disappear any minute now.

'Hmmm, yes, Chechi. They are...just like yours....'

What are they? What are we?

I hold my breath so hard in anticipation of the answer to my unasked question that my stomach hurts. Mani's girls, what are they? Charu and I, what are we? Mani continues to stare blankly at the ground though and I get to see how the night drops quietly over her face. It is like the curtain on the school stage, only that one is heavy red velvet.

I badly need to sneeze; it is the sharp smell of onion peels. Instead I bite off the top of a fingernail. Amma must have used a whole lot of onions for the curry she has made for dinner. I remember noticing they had started to rot in the basket.

'When is our Charumol's school-day, Chechi? Do you need any help? Tell me if you want any stitching done...I can take it home and do it. We've got electricity again at home, they've repaired the line.'

This time I cannot hear Amma reply because I have slipped out of my hideout. I do know that Mani is hoping to make some money out of this too. She is so very, very clever. Amma too knows this and will know what to say.

I want them to stop talking. Now. I want to be free

to run to our room, go throw pillows at our sweet Charu. Scold her for getting simple sums wrong as she has often done this week and for spreading her books all over the bed and floor. Half that room is mine. More than half because I am older, I am the one who will soon go to college, get an engineering degree and start earning more than our mother. I am the one who needs more space because I have more books, more worries in my head. Our family counts on me! What does Charu know except that she is playing princess in a silly school play? She is just a baby while Amma needs me to grow up fast. Really fast so we can hire a proper maid, travel by taxi everywhere, buy fresh groceries from nice stores, go for movies, eat at restaurants without worrying about the bill, go on a vacation to somewhere nice just once in a while.

Everything is so quiet and still in the house, I can even hear the tap dripping in the sink back in the dark kitchen. Amma will hear me if I raise my voice now...she must have anyway sensed I was listening. She can look at my face and make out things. She says Charu can keep a secret much better than me. Charu can act, which is why she is in the play. While I'm the one Amma says things to, if you don't count Mani. I want them to stop talking...so I can go in and tease and scold Charu...pull her braids and push her books off my bed. Order her to start homework. Pick up my Computer workbook and try some advanced exercises, show off my work to Amma and Charu—

In two weeks, my sister will not be a princess. She'll have to stop wearing kajal to school then. Amma would have paid off some loan instalments, Mani would have paid her rent. Her daughters will be safe and fine, just as we will be too. We will go out that Sunday and get ice cream from the new parlour at the junction. Charu, Amma, and I will walk back together, sharing ice creams and licking our sweet, cold fingers clean of the last melted creamy drop. And we will definitely buy a laptop next year. I dream of all this that night and at the end of the dream, the sun falls from the sky.

Again!

The crows wake up immediately and come flying down with their black beaks wide, wide open. I can see the fleshy insides of their mouths gleaming red this time. I can see their flapping tongues. They dance around, cawing harshly, endlessly. The mango tree shivers and sheds leaves; the spot where the sun lies on the ground turns blacker than crows' feathers—

Charu, Amma, and I are fine in the dream, though. We are always fine.

THE THIEF'S FUNERAL

MOHAMMAD SALMAN

Everyone was happy when the Thief died.

It was the postman who had found her, sitting in her armchair behind the unlatched main door, eyes closed as if asleep. In that peaceful tableau, a reign of terror had come to an end.

For sixty years, the Thief held sway over Bijliya, a little hamlet of barely a hundred houses. Over the greater part of three generations, shopkeepers learned to put locks on their cashboxes, dhaba owners chained their plates and tumblers to the tables, watchmen prowled the orchards and families took care to not let on that they had money and valuables to spare.

This was not easy. Firstly, the Thief operated in broad daylight, her identity known to all. Secondly, you couldn't keep her out. In a place as tiny as Bijliya, she was practically *family.*

Her name was not Thief-like. Shehzadi. Princess. Unless you remembered that it was thieving, plunder, pillage, and murder that made people kings, queens, princes, and princesses in the first place.

Generations came and went as Shehzadi stole money, food, and valuables. The world outside changed over those sixty years. So did the face of the village and the interiors of the houses. But out on the street, the Thief was a constant.

At the stroke of midnight on 15 August 1947, as the world slept, the people of Bijliya awoke to find their pockets picked. In 1962, when the Chinese crossed the border into India, the first Seth of Independent Bijliya noticed a rupee missing from his day's earnings. When Bangladesh was born in 1971, so were new grudges when the travelling Kashmiri salesman found a rug missing from his cart. When men, women, and children in Bijliya cheered the World Cup win in 1983, they didn't notice the cartons of mangoes disappearing from the mandi as they huddled around the Seth's radio. When the villagers tuned into *Kaun Banega Crorepati* in 2000 with their neighbours crowded around their TV sets, Amitabh Bachchan's baritone masked the sounds of chickens being stolen, umbrellas disappearing and plates of drying chillies and papads vanishing into the night. Every few years, the clergy of every religion practised in the village would be at each other's throats, but in their hatred of the Thief, they were all united.

There was little they could do about it, and the people of Bijliya could not put a finger on the *exact* reason. A mild fear festered in the hearts of the men sent to beat her up, growing into sheer terror as they went close, leaving them rather *gentle* behind their robust heft for the rest of their lives. When the Thief walked into a house or a shop, its occupants felt an absentmindedness descend upon them, an inability to resist her demands. After she left, the superstitious totems they strung over their thresholds looked worn, as though they *tried,* but failed.

There were other rumours around the Thief too. Whispered stories of a mysterious skill in healing, of bringing health back where modern medicines failed. But they came from people you didn't listen to if you lived in a pretty little

The Thief's Funeral

village home in a row of similarly pretty homes. There was a word for women who had Shehzadi's alleged powers, but they did not like to speak it. Evil followed that word where it was spoken, or so their ancestors said.

And now she was dead. 'Good riddance!' said Bijliya's notables. But the joke was on them, you know. Bijliya was a place of tradition. The rules required children to bear the tyranny of their parents and eventually become tyrants themselves. There were rules for what you could eat and what you couldn't, how you greeted people, what you said about India's neighbours, who you could marry (and who you couldn't), and who could (or could not) build a new pretty house among the rows of other pretty houses. The people of Bijliya followed these rules to a fault.

On the day the Thief died, an inconvenient rule reared its head. It required every person in Bijliya to be given a funeral, funded by the community. Every single one. There was no way out of it. It had to be done, and it had to be done with dignity and respect.

The Pradhan ordered a collection, going around the village himself, carrying a square wooden box with a little slit on the top. The villagers reluctantly parted with a few notes, each remembering their reasons to hate the Thief.

'She took a quart of milk from me every day! Thirty years in a row, not a day missed! And it cost me twice as much, because she'd take it fresh, before I could take the bucket to the tap!'

'She preyed on my feelings to extort from me. Twenty rupees to carry one letter to the Seth's daughter. Each time! If my dhaba didn't do well, I would have become a pauper before we even married!'

'*Twenty?* You got off cheap, uncle! The love letter service is a hundred rupees a letter these days. I don't know who will replace her, but I will not spend a rupee more than ten.'

There were vegetable hawkers who gave the woman a lifetime's supply of greens, orchard owners with seasonal mango donations that amounted to many crates, and (allegedly) tens of thousands of rupees in lost coins and currency notes.

Shehzadi's reign of terror had followed the same pattern, day after day. Her plunder timetable was as much a part of Bijliya's culture as dowry or the caste system.

She would walk out of her house when the clock struck eight every morning, empty jute jhola in hand. First, she visited the pretty houses, no more than three a day. She kept a roster that allowed families a month to recuperate between extortions. Having collected some food and occasionally, clothes and money in her jhola and the latest gossip in her head, she headed for the bazaar. If it was Monday, she would go to the Seth, the one who owned the big store and the bus that did the daily run to Hardoi, two hours away. She always arrived when the store was at its busiest, and always sat next to him at the counter.

The Seth *hated* her. The old pestilence saw through his conniving, cheating ways, knowing well that he charged the villagers more than what his goods were worth. It was either that or the bus to Hardoi (fifty rupees a ticket, with a bonus bone rattle from the awful ride), so the villagers put up with it.

The Seth deployed four boys at the shop. They helped him service the steady throng of customers and keep an eye on shoplifters. Shehzadi was too quick for them. He was always a few hundred short at the end of the day, and no one could understand how. He had once installed a CCTV

The Thief's Funeral

camera, but voltage fluctuations blew it up. Modern security had nothing on Bijliya.

The Thief would then spend some of her loot at the dhaba, buying a cup of hot, sweet tea to wash down the food collected in the morning, lingering over the meal as cars, jeeps, and buses sped past on the highway. Travellers leaving Bijliya after a quick bite would realize some hours later that the bills didn't quite add up. There was always the odd note or coin missing.

Lunch done, Shehzadi would rest under the peepul tree that nearly covered the entire village square. There she would sit and watch people go by, occasionally talking to the children who played in the cool, comforting shade. Sometimes, the candy-seller from the next village cycled past. On those days, every child got a toffee. Bibi Amma, the children called her. Their children did the same, and so, eventually, did their grandchildren.

As the blazing white sun mellowed, she would start walking through the main street, where an improving life over the decades had led to long rows of tiny but well appointed houses, each painted in bright, cheery colours. Young women and men with cameras came from as far as Lucknow and Delhi to take pictures. *Model village*, they called it.

The Thief herself lived half a kilometre beyond the edge of the village, in a two-room cottage at the centre of an unkempt patch of land surrounded by a waist-high mud fence. A forest grew within this little patch, its trees exploding with sound as the starlings came back at the end of day.

Shehzadi would not stop here. Not yet. She would walk a further half kilometre to a dishevelled cluster of houses, completely the opposite of the beautiful main street of Bijliya.

This place was the Dalit basti, home to those who did the jobs no one in the main village wanted to, and were thanked with discrimination for their pains. What Shehzadi did there was a mystery. No one dared ask.

'Perhaps she steals from them, too,' the Seth used to say. 'No discernment.'

His shop boys, who lived in the basti, would smirk and say nothing. They weren't the ones struck dumb with fear when Shehzadi came around to the shop. They weren't the ones worried about hidden evil powers lying in wait, eager to strike.

You could set your watch by the Thief's movements.

∽

The Pradhan's collection box was heavy by the end of the day. He'd covered all the houses in the main village. A gold ring in his left ear sparkled as the setting sun set it aflame.

'You haven't been to the Dalit basti,' his deputy said to him. 'They might have a contribution to make.'

The Pradhan grimaced at her. 'I...don't go there. You know I never do.'

'Shehzadi *did*, sir. You're sending the wrong message. She was part of their lives.'

'I am *not!* Not in the way she was, at any rate. I am mindful of the people I am seen with.'

'Even so....'

'Enough.'

They spent a moment in uncomfortable silence.

'You'll still have some money from them, you know.'

The Pradhan glared at her. 'Why?'

'It's coming to you.'

They looked up at an elderly man walking to them.

The Thief's Funeral

Gaunt, slightly bent, difficult to identify without his grey uniform, which he had discarded for a worn but neat lungi and kurta.

'Dhaniram, what brings you here?' the Pradhan said.

The village's oldest sweeper joined his palms in greeting.

'I heard you were collecting money for the Bibi's funeral, sir. We waited for you.'

'You know I...cannot come.'

'I realized. So we collected the money ourselves. Please accept this from us.'

He reached into his pocket and pulled out an envelope. It was heavier than a ten-house settlement of Bijliya's poorest would have managed.

'That's a lot.'

'It isn't, Pradhanji. Not for the Bibi.'

'Are you sure?'

'Yes. I think this will pay for a tiny stone tomb and a nice headstone.'

'It will pay for more than that. This is very generous of you. Thank you.'

'Not at all, sir. One more thing. Can I speak at the burial?'

'Of course. No one else has volunteered. It will just be the two of us.'

Dhaniram bowed his thanks and went away. The Pradhan took the cash out of the envelope and counted.

'This is a lot of money!'

'Yes,' said the secretary, smiling.

'But why? Do they fear extortion from her ghost?'

'If only you could see past your prejudices, sir.'

The next morning, the Thief was laid to rest in a grave dug right outside her cottage. A will was found, where she left the house to the residents of the Dalit basti, to use as they saw fit. Prayers were said, tears were shed. Shehzadi's foes did well to keep straight, solemn faces. And then it was time for the eulogies.

Trays of samosas, jalebis, and biscuits were laid out on a series of tables joined together in the village school. Bijliya's notables walked in and seated themselves on plastic chairs while the rest of the village sat on dhurries spread on the ground. Children distributed little leaf pattals bearing food. The snacks reached all but a huddled group of visibly poorer people seated at the back.

The Pradhan waited for the hubbub to settle before delivering his eulogy.

'I know our village had a difficult relationship with Shehzadi,' he began, 'but she was one of our elders. There is never an easy relationship with those who have seen a time before ours. Such as she was, Shehzadi was part of this village's soul. There is no memory of Bijliya without her. Some of you may have had...problems with her, but you remember that there was always a laugh to be had when she was around. Nearly all of us remember afternoons made brighter by the toffees Bibi Amma gave us during playtime. Many of us were able to marry who we loved because she carried our letters, though we may have paid through our noses for them. I ask you today to pray that she rests in peace, out of your sense of humanity if not out of grief.'

A perfunctory murmur followed. Dhaniram saw the wealthier citizens speaking most animatedly among themselves, and anger seared through him when he saw the word chor mouthed more than once. He saw the Seth rise.

The Thief's Funeral

'Pradhanji, I believe we must return to our jobs now. It is nice to see us all turned out in solidarity, but surely, we can't waste a day's work mourning a thief?'

Dhaniram was in front of the Seth in an instant.

'Pradhanji,' he said, not taking his eyes off the trader, 'you promised that I would speak today. Could you ask everyone to stay until I've spoken?'

The Seth glared at the sweeper. There was an affront, but it could not be spoken of. Times had changed and the Seth could not have hit Dhaniram as his ancestors had done before him.

'Enough!' he cried, 'Dhaniram may be blind or worse, but the evil that possessed our village is dead now. None of you has the courage to say it, but I will today. Shehzadi's thieving was a cover for a far greater evil. She was a witch. Churail!'

'Sethji!' the Pradhan shouted, 'it does you no credit to talk like that. Let the man speak.'

'It does nobody credit,' said Dhaniram. 'I do not think it matters whether Bibi was a witch or not. There are people who hate her because they are forgetful and ungrateful. And because they do not respect everyone in Bijliya like she did. Shehzadi was the only person who broke bread in every household, and yet I see that it changed nothing. Here we are, at her funeral, but my neighbours are seated right at the back, not offered food at an event that *we contributed the most for,* while the holy men and the rich people of this village are seated in honour and fawned upon. In sixty years, she could not get you to treat us like equals.'

'That does not sound like a eulogy, Dhaniram,' the Pradhan interrupted, 'let us remember what we gathered for, please.'

'I do. Which is why it breaks my heart to see so many of you *rejoice* at her death. I would ask Sethji and his wealthy friends, did Shehzadi's plunder dwarf what you yourselves earned by cheating, corruption, and violence? But that is a pointless question.'

He turned to the rest of the villagers.

'The rich and the powerful have their reasons, but what about you? Look beyond the Thief, and the *witch,* and speak to the elderly among you. Shehzadi was a girl once, and there are those here who remember her with great love. Grandfathers ruling over piles of brick and mortar, who wonder daily, *what might have been?*'

He smiled as he saw three pairs of eyes moisten.

'You remember that her love wasn't yours to command. At least *you* learned, and raised families capable of true respect and fellow-feeling.

'The children seated here have always known a Bijliya that is popular with visitors—a clean, pretty village that they put on postcards. But was it always so? Your parents seem to have forgotten what Bijliya was like, and how it changed.

'If there was witchery here, it was of a very practical kind. Was it not Shehzadi who told you bananas would grow better on this soil than wheat, and are dozens of you not better off because of that? How many of you were a week away from killing yourselves over small loans, only to find that someone quietly slid the right amounts under your doors? You promised to keep that help a secret, but did any of you realize how *many* people were helped and made to keep the same promise? How many of you were forewarned about illnesses that could have killed your children? And when the hot-headed among us fanned the flames of hate,

The Thief's Funeral

why did guns jam and swords rust *every single* time a riot was on the verge of happening?

'For all this, you grudge her the odd rupee, a little food, and clothes? Why? How many of the wealthy,' and he rounded upon the ones in chairs, 'remember that one big obstacle to their success being cleared away, mysteriously and without explanation? Who remembers that secret loan, that fortuitous meeting, that crucial crop inexplicably protected from the rain? Little mercies for little people, when they had *everything* to lose. In beautifying and painting your homes you have forgotten where this prosperity came from. You have only to travel to the next village to see how lucky you are.'

Dhaniram stopped for a sip of tea. No one moved. He saw tears in many eyes, and shock in others.

'We had a treasure, friends. And today we are poorer. Yet you kept this from the children, speaking only of thieving and witchery. But my basti remembers. We remember that night, thirty years ago, when a group of you wanted to poison our well. Respectable men with happy families, but back then you were *just boys*....'

'Now, now, Dhaniram, there is no need to....'

'You were among them, Pradhanji, *own up to it!*'

'I do! And I will carry that shame till I die.'

'Then stand up and *make this village remember Shehzadi as she should be.*'

The Pradhan turned to face the village, tears in his eyes.

'You are right. My generation may be beyond redemption, *but the children must know.*'

He looked at everyone present, his gaze lingering on the ones seated in chairs, every one of them in shock, their eyes imploring him to adjourn the meeting.

'There were ten of us, drinking in the fields one night. One of us had been denied a college seat. We complained about missing opportunities we deserved, when all around us the children of sweepers, leatherworkers, and landless labourers topped exams, became officers and featured in the papers. We decided to punish their kind by poisoning the Dalit basti's well. The plan stayed in our heads even after we sobered up the next day. We passed word around and found support from many people.'

'Did anyone in the basti know?'

'You found out. We tied you up and hid you in the Seth's shop, and gagged you so you couldn't scream.'

'Did Bibi find out?'

'She did, and she asked us not to do it. We drugged her tea that day and locked her in her cottage.'

'Could you poison our well?'

'No. The morning before the poisoning, the water in our well turned brackish. It was the peak of summer, and there was no water nearby. We were shocked. There is no brackish water anywhere in this part of the world. We could not reach out to nearby villages for help. Only the Seth had a phone, which did not work that day. We tried to send the bus out of the village in every direction but the roads had caved in nearby. Bijliya was stranded without water.'

'Without *appropriate* water, as you saw it.'

'Yes. Everyone was reluctant to drink from your well. But when the children's cries became unbearable, some of us realized what we had done. The others were adamant, but the heat and thirst bent them. We freed you and escorted you to the basti. There we asked everyone in the neighbourhood to forgive us and begged that they share their water. You forgave us in an instant.'

The Thief's Funeral

'And you've kept your hands off us ever since. This village would have fallen to ruin if your plan succeeded. You stayed *human* because Shehzadi made it her business to protect everyone.

'Go back to her grave, *everyone*. And pay your respects honestly this time.'

Dhaniram walked away, to the sounds of a whole village beginning to cry.

A NEW HOME FOR BHAINSA
MADHULIKA LIDDLE

Bhainsa was born the year Ameena turned three. Ameena, clutching Dada's hand, was taken to see the newborn heifer. She stared at the little black creature, and said, solemnly, 'It's a bhainsa.' A water buffalo, no cow at all. Her grandparents and parents, her uncle and aunt, tried to convince Ameena that cows only bore cows, not buffaloes, but Ameena stuck to her guns. It *looked* like a buffalo, so a buffalo it had to be. Within two days, the rest of the family capitulated. The cow was named Bhainsa.

And Bhainsa she remained, through the next fourteen years. She calved intermittently, producing milk as and when she did so. The calves always had first right to the milk; the Hussains, after all, were a soft-hearted lot, and Bhainsa was part of the household. A mother, like Dadi, Ammi, and Chachi. You didn't deprive mothers of the company of their children. More importantly, you didn't deprive children of their nourishment. If Allah thought fit to bless Bhainsa with calves, and the calves could never quite finish the vast quantities of milk Bhainsa produced, thus leaving some milk for the Hussains to drink, to pour into their chai, or to churn into butter and boil into ghee...well, that was the mercy of Allah at work. They were grateful.

In any case, it was not as if Bhainsa was bred for milk: the family made their living from their fields of sugar cane, not from cowsheds. Back in the days of the British, when Dada had been a boy, the Hussains had had a dairy. But because Dada liked sugar cane farming more than dairy work, the cows had dwindled away. When Bhainsa's mother died, she was not replaced. Neither were the others. Bhainsa's calves, once weaned, were sold off.

It had been three years since Bhainsa had last calved. Ameena's cousin Shahrukh, whom Dada had named after a prince but who had ended up modelling himself after some paltry filmwallah, came home from Kanpur, where he worked in an office. He sipped his tea and gazed thoughtfully at Bhainsa as she lay under a neem tree, placidly chewing the cud.

'She's not going to give any more milk, is she?' he said.

'No,' said Dada, fondly fluffing out more grass in front of the cow. 'She's too old to bear any more calves.'

'Then get rid of her,' Shahrukh said nonchalantly.

Shahrukh's remark was greeted with unanimous horror. Dadi began a melodramatic tirade. Ameena's father spat out a muffled curse and Chacha, embarrassed at his son's faux pas, muttered something about the younger generation having no respect for values.

'I'm not saying you should kill her,' Shahrukh explained. 'Just don't keep her any more. It's a waste of time and money.'

'Bhainsa is a member of the family,' Dadi whispered in a voice thick with emotion. 'Will you throw us out when we get too old?' The tone had gone from piteous to reproachful. Shahrukh's mother, Ameena's Chachi, jumped to her son's rescue, but without conviction. 'We're not cows, Amma! That's not what he means!'

Shahrukh ignored the attempts at emotional blackmail. He let the reproach and the accusations slide by. Finally, he attacked their stubborn love for the creature with hard fact. Bhainsa would grow older and weaker. She would need medical attention—and where would they get that, here? He overrode their assertions that they were perfectly capable of looking after sick animals.

At last, he played his trump card. 'And what happens when she dies?' he demanded. 'Will you take her into the field and cut her up?'

There was an uproar at that. Dadi burst into tears, Chachi began crying at having given birth to such a debauch, and Chacha reprimanded Shahrukh for thinking them such barbarians as to eat one of their own kin.

'Of course not,' said Shahrukh in his unruffled and utterly infuriating way. 'I didn't say you'd eat her. But what would you do with her?'

That flummoxed them. Till some years earlier, one never thought of that. Dead cattle were attended to, their horns, hooves, hides, and bones going their legitimate ways, to legitimate uses. To faraway factories and industries where they were converted, or so Shahrukh told them, into things that never even made their way into the villages. Few people kicked up a ruckus about a dead cow.

No longer.

'Especially since we're Muslim,' said Shahrukh ominously. 'A Muslim with a dead cow? They'll say we killed her for beef.'

'They wouldn't!' screeched Chachi. 'Everybody in this village knows us. They know we love Bhainsa! Why would we kill her?'

'You don't know what's going on,' Shahrukh said. 'There are bands of gaurakshaks going around, and their motto is to kill first and ask no questions later. They're all over

A New Home for Bhainsa

the place, and they won't ask the neighbours if you loved your cow. They'll lynch you first.'

He spent the rest of the evening telling them all he knew. Some, though they did not know it, was embellished with a view to increasing its impact. Some was, though Shahrukh himself did not know it, rumour.

All of it served just one purpose—to persuade six indignant and stubborn people that it was all for the best if their beloved cow was sent off.

'But where?' Dada finally said, and Shahrukh heaved a silent sigh of relief at what seemed to be the first sign of capitulation. 'To a gaushala,' he replied. 'Send her to a gaushala and they will look after her. They'll drink her piss and put garlands of flowers around her neck.'

'They won't hurt her, will they?' Dadi asked, and Shahrukh assured her that they would not. Dadi looked unconvinced.

The problem, though, was far from solved. More obstacles loomed now.

First of all, how would they take Bhainsa to the gaushala?

'Why should there be a problem with that?' asked Chacha. 'We can borrow Mohsin's tractor-trolley.'

That was what they always used when a dozen or so of them had to travel anywhere further than the old people could go on foot, or if they had to transport something bulky. The sugar cane, when harvested, was taken to the sugar mills near Modinagar in it. When Mohsin's nephew got married in Hapur, most of the older and more fragile members of the family had travelled in it, while the younger and more able-bodied had gone by bus.

Shahrukh shook his head. 'Just like that? In the daytime? They'll think you're a cattle smuggler.'

'At night, then.'

'No, no! That will be suicide. They will be even more suspicious if they catch you in the night.'

'What is happening?' asked Ameena, who had come in just then from her home at the other end of the village with her two-year old. She was divested of the child by her mother, who was relieved to have found a legitimate reason to escape a discussion so harrowing. Ameena was brought up to date on all that Shahrukh had said.

'What is this about that she can't go by day and she can't go by night?' Ameena snapped at her cousin. 'This sounds like the story of Narasimha. That demon who couldn't be killed during the day or at night, inside or out, by man or by animal. So Vishnu took on the avatar of Narasimha to kill him at twilight, was it, on a threshold?' Ameena had topped her class in Hindi all through school, and was proud of it. She revelled in showing off her knowledge not just of the language but of the Hindu scriptures that had been mandatory reading in higher secondary school.

Shahrukh made a face at his cousin, but it didn't deter her. 'And you, I suppose, will be Narasimha,' she said in her snide way.

Shahrukh thought it beneath his dignity to respond to that jibe. He ignored Ameena and turned instead to his father. 'We'll have to find some other way to take her to the gaushala. Not in Mohsin's tractor-trolley.'

'Why do you think I called her Bhainsa?' Ameena butted in. 'Because she looks like a buffalo. Same colour. Just glue a tuft of hair on her head, make a fake nose—chart paper, cut out and painted, will work well—and she'll pass off as a buffalo.'

They stared at her, Shahrukh with fury, the others with mingled respect and hope and annoyance.

The minutes went by. Dada was looking harassed by now, as were his two sons. Dadi was weeping, and Shahrukh's mother was trying to calm her down. Finally, just as Dada was sinking deeper into his habitual slouch, getting ready for a nap, Shahrukh spoke up. 'I have an idea,' he said.

∽

Shahrukh was gone the rest of the day. He returned at night, looking tired but mysteriously jubilant. He refused to say what he had been up to. 'You'll see,' he said, as he washed his hands and sat down to dinner. Nothing, not the entreaties of his mother and aunt, the queries of his father, or even the threats of his uncle and grandfather, could prevail upon Shahrukh to drop even a hint of what he had in mind.

The next morning, Shahrukh had barely wolfed down some roti and a cup of tea before he was gone again. 'What *is* he doing?' Dada asked, of no one in particular. No one answered him; no one could.

Three hours later, when Shahrukh's father and uncle were away in the fields, Shahrukh returned, on his back a large, shapeless sack. He hurried past the whitewashed brick wall, past the straggly marigolds that flanked the door, their dried flower heads drooping like hopeless mourners at a funeral. He banged with the metal chain on the outside of the door and called, but he need not have: Dada, springing up from the charpoy in the courtyard, opened the door before either of his daughters-in-law could emerge from the kitchen.

Five minutes later, Shahrukh's father and brother, summoned from the fields by Dada—who could bellow like a bull when he wanted to—had arrived. So had Ameena, drawn by some strange intuition: Shahrukh suspected she had been lurking in the vicinity, waiting for news.

The family gathered around. The only sound was of Bhainsa mumbling gently to herself under the neem tree. Eight necks craned as far as they could go. Eight pairs of curious eyes watched as Shahrukh undid the sack and drew forth a mass of cloth, glittering with sequins, tinselled and beaded and covered in rows of little seashells.

Ameena was the first to react. 'What is that?' she said. 'It looks like a lehenga.'

Shahrukh grunted. 'You *would* see a lehenga. Of course, it's not. See—,' and he shook it out. It still did not make sense, a large rectangle of eccentrically decorated cloth. And not a proper rectangle either, but one with odd protuberances in places, and with two carefully symmetrical holes at one tapering end.

It was not until Shahrukh had also pulled out some more lengths of cloth, a faded saffron in colour, that Ameena breathed, 'Ya Allah. It's one of those sadhu-like fellows who go around with a cow, asking for alms.'

'It's not the sadhu,' Shahrukh retorted, smug. 'It's the clothing. For the man and the cow. I will be the sadhu and Bhainsa will be the cow.'

There was utter silence for about ten seconds. Ameena's toddler stirred in her arms. The cow belched.

'You moron!' Chacha whipped off his chappal and aimed it at his son's head. Shahrukh leapt nimbly out of range, but his livid father was equally nimble. 'Are you out of your mind? You will dress up like a sadhu, will you? And you'll drape these—these carpets—on our cow?'

A New Home for Bhainsa

Shahrukh, dodging the chappal and the blows, took shelter behind the women of the household.

'At least listen to me!' he yelled, over the furore of his father's anger, the pleas of his older female relatives, and the infuriating giggling of Ameena. 'At least listen!'

But Chacha was not in a mood to listen. And by then, neither were Ameena's Abbu nor Dada. Abbu was angry, too, at having been called home from the fields before they could finish their work. 'You come with us,' he told Shahrukh. 'Come and help finish the work you made us leave midway—' but Chacha interrupted him, saying that this worthless son of his could not be depended upon to do anything correctly. He would ruin their fields.

It was Dadi, gentle and submissive, who spoke up. 'Why don't we discuss this in the evening, when you're all back?' she suggested. 'We will see then how believable Shahrukh and Bhainsa look in their disguises. Yes?'

Ameena was the only one dissatisfied with the suggestion. Even as Abbu and Chacha hurried back to their fields, she grumbled to Shahrukh, 'Why can't you show me now, eh? I can't keep coming here every few hours. My mother-in-law will have my hide for it.'

'What, just for you? I should put on all of this for you?' Shahrukh stared. 'What do you think this is, the trailer?'

'And you're Shahrukh Khan, of course,' Ameena sneered.

But she had her way, and both Shahrukh and Bhainsa—the latter her usual placid self—donned their costumes in the relative privacy of the yard behind the house. Dadi, Ammi, and Chachi gathered around. 'Bhainsa looks so pretty,' murmured Chachi affectionately.

'You don't look like a sadhu,' Ameena said.

'What do you think a sadhu should look like? There are sadhus today with smart phones and gelled hair,' Shahrukh shot back, with all the belligerence of a saffron-clad champion of cows.

'You could pass off as a sadhu,' Ammi conceded. 'With some ash and some sandalwood paste on your forehead. You'll have to practice all the words they say, and the way they behave, though. How will you do all of that, in so little time? You need to return to Kanpur.'

'Bhainsa will die of old age before that,' said Ameena cuttingly. 'In any case,' she added, 'everybody in this village will recognize you and Bhainsa, disguise or no. You can dress up all you want.'

'So what. I'm not scared of the villagers anyway. Wasn't Dada saying that everybody knows how much we all love Bhainsa?'

'But you said,' butted in Dadi, 'that the gaurakshaks were everywhere.'

And since that was what he had said, and since the combined reactions of the female members of his family were later mirrored in the reactions of his male relatives as well, Shahrukh had to abandon the idea. With many dark looks at his family and much grumbling, Shahrukh replaced the borrowed costumes in the sack—Dadi remarked wistfully that poor Bhainsa looked very bare without the fine caparison—and said he would return them to their rightful owner the next day. He spent that night tossing and turning and arose bleary-eyed and grim-faced. He drank his tea in silence, refused breakfast, and left home even before the other men had set off for the fields.

A New Home for Bhainsa

The Shahrukh who returned a few hours later was a different man, his step light, his swagger pronounced and his grin so radiant that it made Dada regard him with suspicion. 'What now?' Dada growled.

'I have found the perfect solution,' Shahrukh breathed. 'There can be nothing better than this. For us or for Bhainsa.' He saw Dadi's curiosity drifting into impatience, and hurried to explain. 'Chaturvedi Sahib,' he said. 'Gaurishankar Chaturvedi, who has bought most of Bhainsa's calves all these years. Didn't he once say that when his cattle get old, he sends them to a gaushala he owns? Near Pilkhuwa, I think?'

Dada sat up, eyes shining with interest. 'Did he? Are you sure?'

'I remember him mentioning a gaushala,' Ameena's Abbu said, from the corner of the courtyard, where he was preparing Dada's hookah. 'I don't know if it was in Pilkhuwa, but it could have been.'

Chacha was still out in the fields. Shahrukh volunteered to take his lunch out to his father, and to tell him of his brilliant idea. 'Dada and Tau approve,' he said, watching his father's face as Chacha washed his hands and settled down under the mango tree to eat.

'As long as you don't make me look foolish,' Chacha said. 'By now everybody in the family thinks you're a good for nothing, all hot air.' But he did not sound resigned, as Shahrukh had feared he would. He sounded pleased.

So that evening, Chaturvedi Sahib, summoned by Dada, came to the Hussains'. His dhoti was beautifully starched and his turban pristine. He listened to all that they had to say— or all that Dada, as patriarch and designated spokesman, said—and then he asked to have a look at Bhainsa. Which, as Dada later said, was idiotic, since Chaturvedi Sahib was well-acquainted with Bhainsa. Even after he had bought her last calf three years earlier, he had come visiting several times, and had made it a point each time to have a close look at Bhainsa.

This time too he gazed thoughtfully at her, his hands clasped behind his back and lips pursed beneath his moustache. He made a wide circuit of where she sat under the neem tree. He bent and peered into her eyes and Bhainsa looked back at him with her limpid bovine gaze. He lifted her tail—why, Shahrukh could not guess—and tapped on her hooves and her horns. 'She's old but she's healthy,' he said finally, straightening up.

'Of course,' Dada said, affronted. 'We've looked after her as if she were our own child.'

After much hemming and hawing and exaggerated pondering, Chaturvedi Sahib announced that he would take Bhainsa to his gaushala. The announcement was received with a collective sigh of relief, and Shahrukh puffed out his chest just that little bit more.

The next half hour was spent working out the logistics. When Bhainsa would be taken away. How she would go. The family, perturbed by all the horror stories Shahrukh had told them, were anxious. Would Bhainsa be safe? What vehicle would Chaturvedi Sahib use? Would she be able to lie down in it, wondered Dadi—Bhainsa was old and couldn't stand for long.

Chaturvedi Sahib was patient and polite. He assured them that Bhainsa could not be in better hands. He would bring a tractor-trolley, and Bhainsa could lie down in it, if she wished. Yes, a load of grass could be sent along with her for the journey. He wasn't sure if he'd take her to the Pilkhuwa gaushala or to another one. He owned

A New Home for Bhainsa

several gaushalas, dotted across the area. He would make the arrangements.

Ameena, when she came by the next morning, was given the news. Shahrukh, still smug about his victory, told her the whole story. How he had found an intelligent solution to the problem. How it took an educated, aware and clever man to find the answer to a problem that had plagued an entire household for so many days.

Ameena was gracious enough to congratulate her cousin. 'As long as Bhainsa is fine,' she said philosophically.

Two days later, Chaturvedi Sahib arrived with a tractor-trolley driven by one of his men. The cow, after being fawned over and cried over by various members of the family, was loaded onto the tractor-trolley. Besides the fresh-cut grass that was placed in front of Bhainsa by way of a snack, she was fed a couple of rotis and a lump of gur. And then, with Chaturvedi Sahib sitting in front beside the driver, the vehicle drove off, bouncing along the rutted dirt road.

'Well, that's done,' said Shahrukh. 'See? All it took was some enterprise.'

That same evening, he too left the village and went back to Kanpur.

There was the occasional phone call to or from the family, mostly from. Chachi phoning to check if her son was well, when he would be coming home next, and whether he was eating properly. Chacha phoning to ask for some help with a convoluted and potentially worrying letter received from the co-operative bank. Ameena's Abbu, needing some information about an acquaintance who might be able to get Ameena's husband a job in Lucknow.

Then one day, a WhatsApp message arrived. It was from Ameena, the only relative back in the village who was tech-savvy enough to use WhatsApp. It was a news article. A small piece of news, very local. Gaurishankar Chaturvedi, local councillor and very active gaurakshak, had been arrested on charges of cow smuggling. It had been discovered that his many gaushalas were mere conduits: the cattle went right on from them, off to varied industries. Buttons, gelatin, leather, beef exports....

Shahrukh did not go back home to his village for the next year.

RETURN TO LIFE
MUDDASIR RAMZAN

In his sleep, Ghazali dreams about his return to life:
He had just returned from the university when his wife Qurat told him about her pregnancy. They were delighted that finally they would have someone who would bring joy to their lives and would restore their stature. They renovated their double-storeyed house, requested their parents (both Ghazali's and Qurat's) to stay with them, to which they happily agreed. There was happiness all around them. It was a dream come true. Ghazali redesigned his study; he wanted to have shelves of children's literature for his coming child. Those were the most beautiful days for him. When Kabir was born, it seemed to them that God had given them everything. Though there were visible traces of Ghazali in his son's appearance, he could see that Kabir is much more intelligent and a cure to what Ghazali lacks in himself. Giving him the best of education, Ghazali and Qurat have been overjoyed every time they heard well of their son. Any parent would be. Kabir was soon considered the ideal child, and every single person he met was proud of him.

Meanwhile, he had awakened; the memory of Kabir's death overwhelmed him. Again, he felt the pain of losing Kabir and Qurat. He wanted to kill himself to be with them in the afterlife; but his religion forbade him. He drifted into sleep again. In his dream, he saw his son and his wife in a beautiful garden, happy and playing with celestial objects, waiting for him to join them. Ghazali wanted to see the calm face of his wife and the youthful gaze of his son again before he was finally awake.

∽

Ghazali was the Chair at Cambridge Divinity College when he was invited to join the mission: to extend his teachings of religion to the people living in the artificially built world on Mars. At first, he didn't warm up to being a part of this evangelical project, but after giving it some thought, he understood the need. He was looking forward to becoming a member of something transcendent. To encourage the dreams of his only son—who was an astrobiologist—and to fill the emptiness that followed the death of his wife, he chose this new life. It was also a chance for him and his son to perform the Hajj which otherwise was not possible. The government of Saudi Arabia, like every other country, has closed the doors for people of other nations. They are not letting people of other lands enter their home even for the pilgrimage. It has taken a heavy toll on refugees, and workers who were transported from the Third World countries. It was also made clear to the people chosen to stay on Mars that they could never return to Earth; even if the restrictions are removed, they still can never perform the Hajj once they land on the new planet. The mixed raw metals melted at boiling temperatures were settled on the Martian crust. Underneath, where humans live to escape from the dangerous atmosphere, Ghazali felt that there was still a possibility for his return to life—to Earth. Residing beneath the ground on this new planet, with every modern facility conceivable, has made him aware of his nature and that of those who surround him. No matter how much people hide their dark side, it'll emerge again, more rigorously, as if taking its revenge; beside it's only the desire for new experiences that offer pleasure, not actually getting what you desire. He still has a will, a passion, to die on the land where he was born, and which, he considers his home, despite having a separate house of his own on the new planet. Unlike here, where he is a machine—perhaps a bit more than a machine with his emotions, dreams, and nostalgia. His new robotic home could not make him feel at home. But how could he possibly travel back to Earth? He was conscious of surveillance satellites wheeling through the human-made sky. This fantasy of escaping from an escape is restricting him from living in his new world.

They were witnessing storms, this time more than usual. Overnight, the temperature had climbed vertiginously, almost melting the veneer of all the iron-made compartment from outside. Ghazali opened his eyes in the middle of the night, finding himself drenched in sweat. The alarm made him stay indoors, where conditions were favourable for survival. He imagined that others would stay home too; so he doesn't have to worry about going out for community meetings and prayers. In this new home, he recalled, lived, and outweighed the stillness of his dreams for another forlorn territory— his youth and the world left behind. At first, there was novelty in this new life, in this other world. His faith, which led him to this new life, was now diminishing in strength. Was it because he was wary of doing the same religious exercises again and again? His faith was holding him like the loosened button of a shirt, waiting to fall. He is well aware of it. He wants to bind it again, sturdily, to keep it fixed, forever, as he has done it many times before. But is there any faith when accompanied by doubt? Even if suspicion is far less compared to belief, the human self can keep only one thing at one time—either doubt or faith. Both don't exist together. Doubt was unsettling him as quickly as faith held him together. A strange situation—where doubt becomes faith—loomed large over him. Is there anything as bizarre as losing a summer of your life in something you consider a trap?

He still dares to fight for his dream, to go back to the place he thinks will make him feel better. But this is all inside him, he's not ready to pour it out. For the community he's representing, he still plays the role that was ascribed to him. After living a good part of his life learning and teaching his religion, a spark of doubt entered his belief. Without warning, this spark engulfed the entire sanctuary of his faith, wherein now rests the residue of his complete total faith. However, doubting his doubt rekindled confidence in him, and he's hoping this spark will reignite complete faith, so he's trying not to think about it. Living among robots has had its effects: he's overlooking the fact that humans cannot control their thinking.

He's leading the prayers of a small group of rebel Muslims, on their request, in Community 786, located to the north of the colony. This small group was an offshoot of a bigger group—who had joined from the different parts of Earth, to serve Islam in the new world. To validate their claim that man (human) is the vicegerent of God not on Earth alone, the senior ulemas united. They felt neglected in the race to inhabit the new worlds. A team of Muslim scholars, along with many other Muslim intellectuals from every field—be it astronomy, medicine, philosophy, physics, politics, art—were selected and sponsored by the rich to spread the word of Allah on the new planet.

The group had their task cut out. One among them was to build a Common Mosque for all the Muslims for the new world, which they did. But they couldn't prevent the group from splitting. The same issues that divided Muslims on planet Earth dogged them. For example, some members of the colony rebelled against the rule that five times daily prayer was necessary, asserting that only once or twice is enough; they also thought of reducing the number of fasting days. Due to time difference they were told to fast for two months, instead of the usual one month observed on Earth. Ghazali supported this rebel group. And this is how he became the imam of a fraction of the people who later built a separate mosque to avoid more fights, not as prominent as their Common Mosque, but sufficient for this group.

The unexpected rise in the temperature was due to a rupture in their apartment caused by some blasts at night. Rumours swirled that aliens had attacked. Ghazali's head reeled with shock when he heard that it was to south of the colony, the part where Kabir's lab was located. Kabir was working in his lab late at night when something hit, and he couldn't escape. The people of the community couldn't move outside. The Technical and Information Department had directed them to wait until the breach was closed. After a while, when it was brought under control, they went to check outside. Concerned for Kabir, Ghazali informed others in the apartment and led the group to check on him. What they saw shocked them; Ghazali collapsed, completely shattered. The lab had all been burnt down. His colleagues found Kabir's right arm, identified by the ring on one of his fingers. That's what was left of Kabir. The devastated father could bury only a part of his son.

People falling from heaven would be angels, comforted the community. Ghazali cursed himself as a failed Daedalus, who, like Icarus, didn't help Kabir and let him burn. Later, the discovered that the cause of the devastation was a space fireball or a meteor, not an alien attack. His son's death caused a haunting that assembled in the corners of the cosmos of Ghazali's reason and emotion. He seemed to be drowning in his guilt, a regret that it was his decision (or his approval) to be a part of the project that proved disastrous for him and his son.

Of late, he has been delving into the existential questions that used to bother him when he was a teenager. Why would this happen to him, he thinks, when he has lived all his life according to the divine plan? These questions had vanished when he had later immersed himself in studying Islam. He now wonders why he is feeling again as he did back then when the doubt created a void in him, and he becomes restless. Was it because he has lost his only hope, his son? Was it his regret? Or, maybe God wasn't of any help to him? Or, does God exist in the first place!?

Life is futile, he thinks. It was not the influence of reading existential and absurd literature, but his own experiences of life. Why does tragedy always follow piety? He compares his life with his less pious colleagues—they are much are much better placed in strategic positions, and relatively happier. He imagines if he were like them, his dear ones would have stayed with him. Whenever he encountered these thoughts his belief came to the rescue: that there is an outstanding eternal life awaiting the pious. But now, he couldn't stop wondering otherwise. The more he thought, the guiltier he felt. Has he lost it all? He thinks: what if this was his only life and what if there's no afterlife, no heaven, no God....

Return to Life

How different it all could have been if he were otherwise, without any faith. The experience he was so proud of suddenly turned against him. Simple living, which he considered a bliss, is a trap for him now. The greatest tragedy is that he cannot tell anyone about the rebellion churning within, not even his closest companions. He fears he will lose them too. What could happen if the people he represents discovered his sudden disbelief? Would they kill him? Or, will they silently remove him from the mission (which is what he wants)? How would his life be then? Alienated, as he is now, and wanting to escape? Will the people on Earth accept him, anyway? He has his anxieties about this. To escape from the futility of his life, he went to perform his duty—to offer prayers, actually to lead them.

In the discussion group, after the prayers, he silently listened to the other speakers who stressed the belief in the One. Thinking what he thought a while ago, a strange emotion overwhelmed him—he had committed blasphemy. He knew it could lead him to hell. That didn't worry him. What bothered him was in the inferno of Hell, he wouldn't be able to see his family, who were pious and are in Heaven. Tears rolled down through the silver strands threaded through his cropped dark beard; others thought he remembered his son. He left silently.

HER DAY
SANTANU DAS

Today was her birthday. She looked at the calendar and asked herself, was it her birthday? Had she forgotten her own birthday? She turned her eyes at the date blankly, stared at the letters like a statue. Something told her that the date was familiar. She tried to think. Her eyes moistened as she remembered. She breathed heavily. A strange calm settled upon her, she stood there, staring at those letters, as if they resembled something dead. Something lifeless, like her mother.

It has been a long time.

Her vision seemed to fade, and in the next instant she found herself crying. Cupping her face with her pale palms, she opened her dimmed eyes to a burning sensation. She rubbed her cheeks, but tears rolled down, breaking all forces. She looked at her palms. It dawned upon her that she possessed a very ugly palm, crooked and rough. She had an old woman's palm, she thought. Naturally.

She was old. Seventy-nine years old.

How old, helpless, and weak she had become, it dawned upon her now. She is old and dying. She will die soon then, she thought, as if comforting herself. She looked at her palms again. She checked the lines on her left palm carefully. Which one was the life-line? Oh, how could she forget? Her age allowed her to forget things, but she clung on to them, fearing they would abandon her forever, like everyone else. Okay, the topmost line was the one, she recollected. On her left hand, the line stretched itself like a stream, stopping just beneath the forefinger, vanishing like a trickle. What does it signify, she thought, bewildered. How many more years to spend over here, she wanted to know.

She paused her thoughts to turn around, and found herself staring at the mirror, at herself. The mirror, 'aayna' she called it in Bengali, was long and narrow, reflecting her body from top to toe. Though she looked at herself daily—after her morning bath, past her evening prayers, at night for braiding her loose hair—but still felt a bit shocked now, examining her very own presence, unmoved and unblinking. What was so striking about her now? Her swollen feet, the crumpled white sari, the protesting collarbones, the long striking neck, and then her face, she observed herself. She saw something in those eyes which shocked her. It was pity, plain simple pity. Pity at herself, on her state, on everything around her for which she had moulded all her life. Pity on her existence, seventy-eight years of existence. A tough player, she thought.

She knew where she was. In her son's room. Her son, Subodh, was out with his wife and daughter. Subodh was an artist. It was she who had always encouraged Subodh to take up art. That night, they went to the birthday party of his daughter's friend. Sumona, her grand-daughter, had told her friend Kaushiki to invite her parents only.

'You won't feel comfortable there, Dida.' Sumona had told her only that evening, asking if the new skirt suited her.

She looked at the walls, painted a shocking yellow. The room seemed to shine upon her like the sun, dazzling her eyes. She sat on the wooden stool in front of the mirror.

She felt elevated now, and she straightened her backbone, widened her shrunken shoulders. Amused at her foolishness, she thought, 'What an ugly queen!'

She found herself inspecting the accessories on the small wooden space in front of the mirror. A deodrant, a white squarish box beside it, a lipstick, some bangles, and a hair-pin. She picked up the lipstick, held it with her palms, like a precious little gem. She revolved the flat base curiously. A small red circle appeared and its narrow length increased. How she grimaced. All the harmful colour and chemicals entering the mouth and then the stomach. Boroline is far better than this. Deliberating upon its uselessness, she brought it near her lips, to try it once. She succumbed to her temptation, dabbing the red stain on her lower lip and then keeping the precious thing hurriedly back in its place with guilt. She looked now, touching her lower lip with her fingers, slowly. How soft and desirable! Well, she had to admit now that she looked beautiful, smiling to herself.

She then noticed a red bindi on the extreme left on the mirror. Subodh's wife detested the bindi, which according to her, did not suit her personality. Maybe Sumona had tried it and then discarded it there. The next moment she found her fingers scraping it off the mirror, balancing the red dot on the tip of her forefinger, breathing tensely. She knew her limits, that of a widow's. She closed her eyes, reminding herself that she was committing a sin. Suddenly, she imagined herself as a bride. She imagined her face, brightened with charm; her forehead adorned with white patterns, the red bindi looking dignified between her brows. She opened her eyes, aghast, ashamed. Her forehead seemed heavy with the unaccustomed weight of the bindi, but still she withstood all the pain, clutching her sari in despair, astonished at her own courage yet somehow proud of herself.

She heard a knock outside, the sound of the main door lock. She froze. They had come back. If she was found in his room it would be disastrous. She rushed to the door, limping as fast as she could, her backbone bent perennially. She switched off the lights. Downstairs she could hear their footsteps, Sumona's childish voice. She hurried out of the room, closing the door behind her, leaving the room into darkness.

'Maa...?' Subodh shouted suddenly.

Resembling a mourning wail, she managed to whisper loud enough. 'Hain..?' She could feel gooseflesh rising.

Not wasting another second, she rushed to the bathroom. Shutting the door from inside, she gasped for breath as she crouched, sobbing and trembling. The footsteps reached upstairs, stopping outside the door. 'What are you doing inside the bathroom?' Subodh asked.

She found herself struggling to answer. She breathed heavily, asking herself the same question.

'Nothing,' her voice choked. 'Just washing my face.'

'Oh, OK. Come out and have your dinner.' He said huskily, his footsteps treading downstairs.

She crouched on the bathroom floor, clutching her face, sobbing hysterically yet softly, lest the sound reach downstairs.

She finally got up and stood by the wash basin. She turned on the tap and splashed water on her face. The bindi slipped off and went into the sink. Rubbing her lips, she managed to get the colour off. She splashed water until she was satisfied that she was cleansed. Yes, now she looked like herself, she felt satisfied.

She went downstairs, drying her face with the end of

her sari. She entered the room and sat on the kitchen floor, cross-legged, her hands still shaking mildly.

'Oh Dida,' exclaimed Sumona. 'The birthday cake was so huge, and so tasty! We danced and played for so long. We should have brought one piece for you....' she paused. 'Well, leave it. We can order it someday...' her eyes lit up in delight, 'Why, on your birthday itself!'

THE PUMPKIN EATERS
SHALIM HUSSAIN

There was a sudden shortage of pumpkins in the village of X. They did not realize it at first. For many years there had been rumours that the production of pumpkins was decreasing but no one had taken it seriously. Every season the merchants increased the price by ten rupees but no one seemed to mind. If the price of rice could increase by one rupee per kilo every year, it stood to reason that the price of pumpkins would increase by ten times that much. So everyone continued to buy pumpkins. They ate it with fish (large and small), they ate it with meat and when fancy took over, they boiled it with eggs. When the merchants came, there was a rush to hoard as many pumpkins as possible. One man chased all his chickens away and filled the coop with pumpkins. Another sold his cows and their tethers so that he could buy more than his neighbour who in turn had built a tall house 5 × 10 size, raised above twenty feet solely to store pumpkins. Another woman was so enamoured by the smell of pumpkins that she wore one on her head, covered it with a turban and claimed that God had touched her hair. She went around the marketplace in the heat of summer, juice trickling down her eyes, and the fragrance of heaven all around her.

The preachers came. They said that this love for pumpkins was no longer a joke and had turned into an affliction. 'It won't be limited to this village alone,' they said. 'Soon it will spread and both banks of the river will turn into deranged pumpkin eaters.' At first, they were entertained but the love of religion cannot trump the love for pumpkin, so the preachers were booted out. The day the preachers left was also the day the merchants came. More pumpkins came—twenty trucks in fact. The mathematics master had no space for the pumpkins, so he cleared his pigeon coops. He beat the sides of the coop and the older ones flew away. With the same stick he poked the littler ones. I was a little boy then, so I stood under the coop with the hem of my shirt spread out. The baby pigeons fell on my shirt and didn't even move—they must have been only a few days old, you know. They were too tiny to have full feathers. Just the tiny stubborn feathers they had, the ones that grow very close to the skin and are extremely difficult to get rid of. So we took the baby pigeons, all the boys in our gang, and walked to the river. There we lit a fire and killed the pigeons. And then we ate them, half raw, half burnt. Needless to say, we didn't have any pumpkins to cook the pigeons because pumpkin is meant for the older men and we had maybe ten pubes between the five of us.

When the pigeons were evicted from the coop, the elders warned us that something bad was coming. Which civilization evicts baby pigeons for pumpkins, even if they are the firmest, juiciest pumpkins in the whole land? 'Pigeons are the freest birds in the whole world,' they said. 'Pigeons choose where to roost and when to leave. If you make them leave according to your own needs, there is something wrong with you.' The older pigeons flew away with the preachers, all the other pigeons also joined them and the merchants showed up.

First the men ate the pumpkins, then the pumpkins started getting smaller and smaller. We didn't notice it, of course, because we couldn't eat pumpkins anyway and soon matters came to such a head that someone dressed up oranges in pumpkin rind and started selling them in the market. Poor fellow was beaten with his own shoes and driven out, as befits a scamster with such nerve, but the funny thing is that all the camouflaged oranges sold out. We realized that anything with even a hint of pumpkin is essentially pumpkin's brother. So, the discarded pumpkin skin and rind from faraway villages were dried and ground and sold as powder in little plastic packets. In the evening you could see men huddled in corners around the market with a small kerosene lamp between them. If you tapped one of them on the shoulder, they turned back in rage, orange powder smeared on their faces. Then someone said that we should eat pumpkin leaves. The merchants came with leaves—both fresh and dried and they had barely pulled their boats to the shore before they were dragged out and bundles of currency notes were thrown at them. Take the money, take all the money, the older men said, but give us pumpkin leaves. In about a month's time the leaves were all eaten and then the stem and finally the roots. School was closed for ten days because all the teachers came with mud in their mouths. This was mud around the roots of the pumpkin patch. They filled their mouths with it, sucked out all the juices and finally gulped it down with water mixed with pumpkin earth. Pumpkin earth they called it, yes, that I shouldn't forget. It was quite the craze for a few months until the elders sat for a meeting and discovered that there was a solution no one had thought of before.

In the village just across the river a strange thing was happening. This was the village where they grew pumpkins for sale. They didn't eat any of it themselves but always looked at the plants lovingly, so lovingly in fact, that the men and women went to bed with pumpkins on their mind. One fine day a woman gave birth to a pumpkin. It was not like our stories, you know, where a fruit comes floating in the river, a childless couple cuts it open and instead of a tiny seed, they find a healthy baby, the size of a little rat. No, it wasn't like those stories. The woman actually gave birth to a pumpkin. It didn't have any magical powers and all, didn't grow limbs and turn into a hero and all that, just an ordinary baby pumpkin. The woman, out of shame, hid the vegetable in the heap her husband was to transport to the city in a couple of days. He found out though—her belly was flat and it was the only pumpkin drenched in blood. He dragged her to the courtyard and asked for an explanation. 'Have you been hiding a pumpkin under your clothes for nine months?' he asked her. She laughed. 'How was it possible,' she asked, 'that he didn't notice every night he disrobed her?' Besides, did she replace the pumpkin with a larger one every day? And how could she? None of the smaller pumpkins were ever touched. It was only when they were large and ripe that they were plucked.

It was hushed up but then the second unexpected birth happened. The hospital nurse had a baby and it had to be delivered at the hospital, government rules and all, you know. So this doctor is running his hand over her belly and he is surprised. This is the oddest shape he has ever encountered inside a woman. So he calls the compounder who comes and rubs the belly and is also confused. Even the nurse doesn't know. They lay her on the bed and ask her to push. There is a lot of tearing and blood and then the baby rolls out of her and slips past the doctor's hands. The doctor is so confused that he doesn't even try to hold the baby in his hands. The pumpkin lands on the ground, the umbilical cord tears and the nurse falls down in pain. She doesn't know what has come out of her but she has felt something extremely large tear out of her. She is scared that her vagina is torn up to her navel and she touches herself to be sure. No, it's all right. There's no significant tear, a little but that's something the doctor will stitch up well. The helpless doctor, well past middle age and having put twenty years of his life in the business tries to hush up the affair. Nearby women huddle around the woman and protect her from the gaze of men, as women usually do.

But they come home with stories. 'You know what,' they tell other women, and then their husbands, 'so and so nurse gave birth to a pumpkin.' 'Oh come on, say the men, that's crazy talk. Is the baby that ugly? But it's not the nurse's mistake you know. That husband of hers, what a face he has, like someone scrubbed their ass on it. If his baby doesn't look like Nosferatu, what will it look like—Chiranjit?' 'Arrey no,' the women say, 'the nurse gave birth to a real pumpkin.' 'Oh yes,' say the men, 'we know. The last time you said that a man had puked out a snake. The farmer dropped his plough, the fisherman dropped his net, and we all ran to the fucker's house. What did we see, a little earthworm in a puddle of vomit.' 'These men will never understand,' the women say and get back to business.

The next day the barber tells his customers about the crazy story his wife has cooked up. But there is something very interesting going on on the television, so no one pays much attention to him except the pumpkin seller sweating on a stool in the corner. But I am going too slow. You don't need all the details. Anyway, so the pumpkin seller asked the barber if his wife had actually seen the pumpkin and the barber asked him why he was so interested in knowing what his wife said and the pumpkin seller said, 'Well I can ask your wife myself tonight.' The barber was again distracted by the television, so he didn't catch the last words. The pumpkin seller half-smiled at his joke and showed half-relief. Then he straightaway went to the barber's house. He stopped outside the auli wall and said, 'Sister, are you home?' And the barber's wife said she was home. They talked, and the farmer said that you know what, my wife also gave birth to a pumpkin. Within the month the same thing happened to three women. The doctor wrote to Guwahati and asked for a transfer. He didn't want so much bullshit during his last few years at the job. Finally the application was accepted and the chap left with suitcases filled with fish, green vegetables, and pigeons.

After ten pumpkins were birthed, everyone noticed a pattern. Only the third child of a woman was a pumpkin. And since it is not every day that a woman gives birth, even to her first child, the births were not regular. But there was nothing anyone could suggest. What were they going to do with the pumpkins? The first few pumpkins were brought to the elders' meeting at the jute auction market and left there. There they shrivelled in the heat and became almost half the size. That is when the merchants came calling. They saw the dried, sorry state of the pumpkins in the auction yard and called an immediate meeting of the elders. 'What is this?' they shouted. 'Do you people have no sense?' Evidently this was the only village in hundreds of miles where pumpkins existed any more. 'So what do we do with these symbols of our shame,' the elders asked. 'Oh, give them to us and we will sell them for you.' But the men refused. 'Whatever be the case, they said, whether these poor things have no legs or hands, or whether they will ever be able to call us "father" or not, they are still our children. We will not let them go with you.' Then one of the fathers took a merchant aside and said, 'Everything is fine and well, sir, it is impossible for us to sell you our children but...just talking, you know, meaning nothing...just talking, what will we be paid?'

'Land, you fool,' the merchant said. 'They are now selling one bigha of land for one pumpkin.' And the men were stunned. 'Land? So they said to the merchants, 'You can't go back today. We will make some place for you at my place but let us consult with our wives first. After all they are the mothers. They should have a say.' The merchants agreed. That night there was a lot of fishing and the merchants' plates were filled with all kinds of food—fried fish, fish with strips of brinjal, fish head mashed with dal, fish wrapped in gourd leaves and steamed (pumpkin leaves are ideal for this dish but given the situation it was not really possible, you know), fish soured with tomatoes and imli, and all sorts of fried foods. Then at night the men went to the women and said, 'So the merchants have told us this and that, and the dried children that are there in the auction centre can actually be sold for land. Do you agree or do you not agree?' 'Oh, those are pumpkins,' the wives said. 'It's another thing that I will never be able to eat a pumpkin in my life but those are the ones that came out of me I don't know why it came out of me. Do with it what sounds best. I would have been happy enough had you taken it to the backyard and buried it but do me a favour and get rid of it as soon as possible. I am done being reminded of my shame.'

So the men met with the merchants at the auction centre the next day and said, 'Our wives are fine with the sale but we would like to come with you.' 'Of course, you should, said the merchants. Do you think we are here to fool you? What will we do with land? Will we eat it? Come with us, see the land and see if its fine for your pumpkins. If you think it's not enough, we can always negotiate.' So the merchants and the men went on their boats and crossed the river. At the opposite side they saw that the people had become slow and thin. But they were not as skeletal as the visitors were and there was some flesh on their bodies. Even their cheeks were full and their buttocks were large, even those of the men. However, there was something extremely tired about the people, as is the unbearable tiredness of a person who sleeps all day. And so they decided upon a price—one bigha of myadi or village land for one pumpkin, one bigha of tauzi or family land for pumpkin peel, and one bigha of encroached government land for the rind. Thus the deal was concluded.

Within a week the pumpkin eaters had eaten all the pumpkins but their land was gone. This is how one fine morning the older people of the village realized that they no longer had any land, just enough to put their feet on. So they scooped out the land. They dug seven feet deep and struck water. Now water belongs to everyone, so they could, of course, not claim the water under their feet as their own. Instead, they filled baskets with earth, stuffed some in their shoes so that they could claim that where they went was their own land. They went to a new village where they filled waterbodies and claimed small patches of land. I remained. I had no land, no love for pumpkin, and no one to travel with. So the new owners came and set up base here. Both the communities—the one who left here and the one who came decided that the pumpkin experience was something that they would both like to forget. The older community learnt that they could buy pumpkins from Guwahati. So from their new homes they ordered pumpkins and even learnt to grow them. However, they didn't taste nearly as good as the ones the new community had brought. Or was it the pumpkin that they had eaten before they met the new community? By now they were not certain they knew. They got pumpkins from across the river, from cities in India, and from across the seas. None of them felt like the pumpkins they had eaten. After the passage of some more time they got over the desire for pumpkins and looked back at the time with deep nostalgia as I look back at the time when wild ducks laid eggs on the hyacinth and we stole the eggs—how if I entered the river with just one basket and one hour of time I could emerge with the basket fully loaded. The new settlers grew very few vegetables. They grew rice instead and when the rice ripened, they realized that the husk was pure gold. That's how this village got its new name—Under the Shade of Gold. And today when you complain that the people here sold their land for nothing, remember that you are wrong. They sold it for the pumpkins.

NOTES ON THE CONTRIBUTORS

Anuradha Vijayakrishnan is an Indian writer and business professional living in the UAE. Her work has appeared in *Magma*, *Kenyon Review*, *Acumen*, and *Stand Magazine*. Her writings have also featured in anthologies including the *Yearbook of Indian Poetry in English* series. She is the author of the novel *Seeing the Girl* and a collection of poetry, *The Who-am-I Bird* which has been translated into Arabic.

Armaan Verma is a writer from nowhere in particular, although his stories are almost always set in India. He studied Politics of Conflict, Rights, and Justice at SOAS, University of London. His work has appeared in newspapers and magazines like *Condé Nast Traveller*, *The Quint*, *HIMAL Southasian*, and *The Skinny*. He enjoys rock climbing, psychedelic rock, and pointless discussions, and he intends to write frantically for the rest of his life.

C. Jayanthi (Jayanthi Chandrasekharan) has been an English print journalist with the *Times of India* and *Gulf News*, Dubai. Having a PhD in Indo-French bilateral relations, she taught French at Loyola College and was also a guest faculty (French), at IIT Madras, Chennai.

Ipsita Mitra has over twelve years' experience in publishing and journalism. Her debut collection of verses, *Smudged Ink and Other Poems*, was awarded 'Poet of the Year' by

Canada-based Ukiyoto Publishing in 2022. In 2020, her short story 'Bohemian Sailor of the Gulf' was published by Sublunary Editions, a Seattle-based independent publisher. The *Indian Quarterly* (April–June 2021) featured her short fiction, 'Kabuliwala Returns'. She writes on books, culture, environment, and gender. She did her MA in Gender and Development Studies and is currently pursuing her PhD in Gender and Development Studies from IGNOU, New Delhi.

Jobeth Ann Warjri is a writer and researcher from Laitkor, Meghalaya. She is a two-time recipient of the Zubaan Research Grant for Young Researchers from the Northeast. She currently teaches writing at Vidyashilp University, Bangalore.

Juanita Kakoty is a writer with a sociological imagination. Her short stories have been published in national and international platforms like *HIMAL Southasian*, *Kitaab*, and the *Assam Tribune*.

Leisangthem Gitarani Devi works as Associate Professor in the Department of English at Shivaji College, University of Delhi. Having made Delhi her 'home' for two decades now, she continues to intellectually, imaginatively, and emotionally engage with her childhood home Manipur in many ways. A glimpse of her imaginative and emotional tryst with Manipur may be witnessed in the short stories 'When the Wind Whispers' and 'Road to Freedom', published in *Muse India* and *Café Dissensus* respectively.

Madhulika Liddle is a novelist and award-winning short story writer, best known as a writer of historical fiction.

Among her most popular books are the Muzaffar Jang series, featuring a Mughal detective in seventeenth-century Delhi; and the *Delhi Quartet*, a four-book fictional series of which the second book is soon to be published. The first book of the *Delhi Quartet*, *The Garden of Heaven*, was published in 2021 to critical acclaim. She also writes fiction in other genres, such as social issues, black humour, and romance.

Md. Shalim Muktadir Hussain is a writer and academic based in Assam. He has done his PhD from the Department of English, Jamia Millia Islamia, and works as Assistant Professor of English at Government Model College, Borkhola. His books include *Betel Nut City* (2019), a poetry collection that won the RL Poetry Award 2017, *Post-Colonial Poems* (2019), a translation of Kamal Kumar Tanti's poetry anthology and *Asimot Jar Heral Sima* (2020). His works have been included in *The Penguin Book of Indian Poets* (2022), *Sahitya Akademi Modern English Poetry by Younger Indians* (2019), and *Penguin Complete Short Stories of Premchand* (2018) among others.

Mohammad Salman is a writer from Lucknow. His work has appeared in the *Gollancz Book of South Asian Science Fiction*, *Kitaab*, and other anthologies. He is also a contributor to *Comixense*, India's first quarterly comics magazine for children. He has a Bachelor's degree in English Literature from the University of Delhi and holds a Master's Degree in Mass Communication from Jamia Millia Islamia. 'The Thief's Funeral' won the third prize in the *Twist and Twain* short story competition.

Notes on the Contributors

Muddasir Ramzan, an emerging writer and academic, received his PhD in English from Aligarh Muslim University. His doctoral thesis focused on the contemporary realities of Muslims and recent developments in postcolonialism and Islam. His research and creative work have appeared in the *Journal of Postcolonial Writing, Journal of Commonwealth Literature, HIMAL Southasian, Outlook India, The Hindu, Critical Muslim* (UK), and other publications.

Neera Kashyap has published a book of short stories for young adults, *Daring to Dream* (Rupa & Co.) and contributed to several prize-winning children's anthologies. Her short stories have appeared in international journals which include *Kitaab, Mad in Asia, Spillwords, Papercuts, Setu Mag,* and *Borderless*; the Indian journals include *Indian Quarterly, Out of Print Magazine* and Blog, *RIC Journal, Guftugu, Teesta Review, Usawa Literary Review, Muse India, The Bombay Literary Magazine, The Chakkar,* and *Yugen Quest Review*. 'Reflections on a Common Journey' was published in the journal *Mad in Asia*, February 2020, under the title 'Tending Tender Things'.

Poet, artist, and editor **Paresh Tiwari** has been widely published, especially in the sub-genre of Japanese poetry. A Pushcart Prize nominee and winner of Touchstone Distinguished Books Award in 2017, his work has appeared in several publications, including the anthology by Sahitya Akademi, *Modern English Poetry by Younger Indians* released to celebrate 200 years of Indian English Poetry. *Now a Poem, Now a Forest*, his third poetry collection, was published by Red River Publications in 2022. He has co-edited the International Haibun Anthology, *Red River*

Book of Haibun, Vol 1, and the landmark anthology of erotic poetry, *Shape of a Poem.*

Rachita Raj is a New Delhi-based former lawyer who switched gears and worked as an editor at a major publishing house for close to a decade. She continues to help bring stories to life as a freelance editor and writer. You can find her reading and writing horror fiction, trekking in the Himalayas, honing her skills as a trivia buff, and birdwatching in her spare time.

Ranjan Pal is an adventurer in both his professional and personal life. Professionally he has had a rich and diverse record of accomplishments at the leadership level in a variety of fields ranging from investment banking to education. Personally, he now pursues his twin passions for the outdoors and travel writing. His travel pieces appear frequently in a number of top global travel media including *Condè Nast Traveller*, *Travel+Leisure*, *CNN Travel*, and *National Geographic Traveler*.

Santanu Das is a writer, entertainment journalist, and film critic currently working with *Hindustan Times*. When not writing about films, he likes to read short stories and listen to audio books. He lives in Chandannagar, West Bengal.

Sourabh Mukherjee has been recognized as 'one of the frontrunners in Indian crime fiction' (*Mid-Day*) and 'one of the most popular writers of Indian crime fiction' (*Asian Age*). He has written several bestselling true crime and psychological thriller novels as well as short stories in English and Bengali, including 'The Highway Murders', 'The Web of Lies', 'The

Trail of Blood', 'In the Shadows of Death', and 'The Sinners'. His books have won accolades from readers and the national media and are in consideration for screen adaptations. Working in a leadership position in a global technology consulting company in AI and Data Science, Sourabh has also written a popular textbook *Big Data Simplified*.

Subhash Chandra is former Associate Professor of English, University of Delhi. He has published three collections of short stories, viz., *Not Just Another Story, Beyond the Canopy of Icicles, A Game of Dice,* and four books of criticism. His stories have appeared in Indian and foreign journals, such as *Confluence* (London), *Setu* (Pittsburgh), *South Asian Ensemble* (Canada) and others. He is on the International Advisory Board of *Intersections: Gender and Sexuality in Asia and the Pacific*, (Canberra, Australia), *Confluence: South Asian Perspectives*, (London), and *Induswomanwriting.com*

Vikram Balagopal is a filmmaker, writer and illustrator. His first book, *Simian* (HarperCollins, 2014), was a winner of the Best Graphic Novel of the Year Award at Comic Con India. His second book, *Savage Blue* (HarperCollins, 2016), is a contemporary fantasy novel set in India. Born and brought up in Kerala, Vikram now lives and works in New Delhi.